SUMMER AT SUNSET HARBOUR

CP WARD

"Summer in Sunset Harbour"
Copyright © CP Ward 2024

The right of CP Ward to be identified as the Author of this Work has been asserted by him in accordance with the Copyright, Designs and Patents Act 1988.

All rights reserved. No part of this publication may be reproduced, stored in a retrieval system, or transmitted, in any form or by any means without the prior written permission of the Author.

This story is a work of fiction and is a product of the Author's imagination. All resemblances to actual locations or to persons living or dead are entirely coincidental.

BY CP WARD

The Delightful Christmas Series
I'm Glad I Found You This Christmas
We'll have a Wonderful Cornish Christmas
Coming Home to Me This Christmas
Christmas at the Marshmallow Cafe
Christmas at Snowflake Lodge
Christmas at Log Fire Cabins
A Stranger Arrives this Christmas
A Train is Late This Christmas
Welcome Home Again This Christmas

The Glorious Summer Series
Summer at Blue Sands Cove
Summer at Tall Trees Lake
Summer at Harbour View House
Summer in Sunset Harbour

The Warm Days of Autumn Series
Autumn in Sycamore Park
Autumn at the Willow River Guesthouse
Autumn in Sunset Harbour
Autumn at the Oak Tree Cafe
Autumn on Maple Tree Lane

For my mother, Judy

SUMMER IN SUNSET HARBOUR

1
THE BEGINNING AFTER THE END

THE ROADWORKS on Winchester Road were like an unwelcome friend. Some kind of mains-pipe disaster judging by the signs, Josie Roberts could literally see her front door from her position in the queue, but in twenty minutes she'd moved exactly fifteen feet, if you could judge distances by the length of the concrete stones that lined the pavement edge.

She had wanted to make tonight special, perhaps open a glass of wine in her little kitchen for the last time, gaze out at the tiny garden she had so treasured, admire the line of shrubs she had grown from seedlings quietly nurturing into mature plants that framed a small but peaceful patio she had designed herself. She wanted to sit in her bath one final time, listen to the chirping of the birds on the telephone wire outside the window, perhaps feel the soft plush of the pile carpet on the stairs as she descended, sliding her feet in that almost childlike way she always did, enjoying the press of the softened corners on the underside of her soles.

Up ahead, the light turned to green. Josie waited for

the traffic to move, but it stayed stock still, until finally someone a few cars up leant out of his window and hollered at the person in front to get off his phone. With a sudden jerk, the front car lurched out of its position, and the others slowly moved forwards.

Two from the front, Josie ground to another halt.

She supposed she ought to savour her last moments in the car, too, the old Volvo she had owned for fifteen years, and had never really treasured until the moment she was told that selling it was her only option. What difference would three-hundred quid make? She still had a load of her junk in the back, stuff she either had to now throw away or rehome: the umbrella Hilda had given her for her fortieth birthday, which now had a broken spoke but she couldn't bear to throw it away; the box of Scottish biscuits she had bought for Mrs. Gleneagles two years ago before finding out she had died of cancer; the box of nineties indie CDs by bands like Terrorvision, Shed Seven, Reef, The Cranberries, and Sleeper, which she could no longer play because the CD player in the car was broken, and she could never play in the house because her now officially ex-husband was a vinyl enthusiast and considered everything else a sell-out.

Then, somewhere back there, perhaps squashed into a seat pocket, was the thank-you letter from one of her private students who had credited Josie's tutoring for getting her a place in university. She had kept it in her car because it was the kind of treasured keepsake that had tended to go missing during her marriage, and even after her ex had moved in with her replacement, she had never quite felt confident enough to move it into the house.

The light changed again, the person in front immediately hitting the horn almost by default, just in case the owner of the front car dared make the same mistake as the last one. This time, to Josie's relief, she got through the light, and drove the extra couple of hundred yards up the road to her own narrow driveway.

She sighed as she parked outside her house and got out. The drive, once used regularly by two cars, had plenty of space on either side of her Volvo now, but even so, she still found herself cracking open the door gently as though afraid of bumping the other car or the fence that had once belonged to Mrs. Gleneagles. Another of her ex's quirks had been to choose at random which side of the drive he parked on, and despite how frustrating it had been, as she walked up to her front door for possibly the last time, Josie couldn't help but feel a pang of nostalgia.

There had been good days, of course there had. Her ex had never been abusive—unless she counted the times she had slept in the car after being locked out of the house, and that was only because he slept more than the average house cat, and once asleep wouldn't have been able to be woken with Big Ben pealing outside the bedroom window—and he had always treated her well. If there was a way to describe him that made sense it was … fleeting.

She unlocked her door for the last time, looked at the post on the mat for the last time—although she supposed she could still drop round if necessary, but it would hurt too much and she wanted a clean break—then hung her coat up on the hook for the last time.

In the kitchen, she made what was possibly in the single digits of her final coffees at her beautiful old mahogany kitchen table—ten by tomorrow morning would probably be a stretch but she couldn't rule it out—then pulled out her phone and called Hilda.

'It's over, isn't it?' her best friend said by way of greeting. 'You've finally cut off the infected branch?'

'If you're meaning, has my divorce been finalised, then

yes,' Josie said, sighing into her phone, leaning close enough to the coffee for the steam to mist up the screen. 'Everything's official as of today. The house goes on the market tomorrow, and thanks to a little bit of legal shafting, he gets two-thirds of everything.'

'He really pulled a trick on you, didn't he? I told you right at the beginning, that's what you get when you marry a verb. You should always marry a noun.'

Josie couldn't help but smile. Reid. Hilda, twenty years older than Josie and already with two marriages behind her when they had met, had disapproved of her now ex-husband from the start.

'I should have listened to you.'

'I made recordings of all my advice so you can play it back whenever you like.'

'Did you really?'

'No, of course not. Although you'd have nothing to play it on, would you?'

'The first thing I'm going to buy once I get my share of the house is a hammer. There won't be a vinyl record within a hundred yards of me that isn't in pieces.'

'Look on the bright side. You get your name back. Josephine Euphrates made you sound like some kind of invasive vine. Josie Roberts, now that's a tulip name.'

Josie smiled. Hilda Lewisham was a botanist, famous in plant people circles for developing a new variety of rose. Selling it had made her a fortune, which she had promptly donated to tree-planting projects in sub-Saharan Africa. At sixty-five years old, she had travelled the world, appeared in *National Geographic*, chaired international conventions, and won top planty-type awards from a dozen planty-type institutions for both her research and her donations. And yet, for some reason, after a chance meeting at a Pilates class, she had chosen Josie—a tired, troubled schoolteacher with a failed musician as a husband—to be her best friend.

'I've been using Roberts since he left me,' Josie said. 'And to be honest, I never really felt right using his stage name.'

Hilda chuckled. 'What was his real name again?'

'Euphrates-Barnacle.'

'I wouldn't wish that name on a weed. Why don't you go to the press? Surely there's a story to sell?'

'He's not famous enough. And you know, I'm just glad it's over. I mean, I know he moved on years ago, but now I can, too.'

'Have you spoken to Tiffany?'

Josie felt a pang of regret at the mention of her daughter. Off at university in Leeds, Josie was lucky to get a monthly phone call. Reid, who had promised to support their daughter using the divorce settlement, had boasted at the court hearing that he was called once a week.

'No,' she said. 'There's no real point until the poison's run its course, is there?'

SHE MOVED out on a blustery April morning. She packed everything she owned that the cost of her legal bills didn't require her to sell into the back of the Volvo and drove across Bristol from Redfield to Knowle West, where a distant cousin had offered her a flat for a month until she could get herself back on her feet.

The rubbish strewn in the tiny front garden downstairs didn't bode well, and the damp stains on the wall in the kitchen were worryingly fresh, but Josie couldn't stand to stay in her old house while she waited for it to be sold. Too many memories, too much turned sour, and too many regrets. She needed to make a clean break, even if 'clean' was a misnomer, judging by the dust collecting in the corners of the flat's poky living room. The view through the grimy window of the charred frame of a burnt-out townhouse was hardly memorable either, but with no curtains, all Josie could do was pull the threadbare sofa around so that it faced the inner wall. That she quickly discovered the corpse of a mouse underneath was probably a good thing; she was able to dispose of it before she needed to go hunting for the source of the smell.

Still, she had to be grateful. She had a roof over her head, even if it was leaking in a couple of places, and the heating worked, even if the immersion heater in the hall gave off a gassy smell. Just in case, she opened the kitchen window a crack, brushing away a few dead flies in the process. The water in the taps ran brown for a few seconds before going clear, but that was okay: she had brought a bottle of wine with her to toast the end of her marriage.

Covering the sofa with the blanket she had kept in the back of her car for those times Reid had locked her out—just in case there were any mice nests hidden down among the springs—she poured a glass of wine, sat down in her new—old, very, very old—lodgings, and lifted the glass.

'To the future,' she said to no one, trying to sound positive while refusing at the same time to cry.

2

A POSSIBLE CHANGE IN FORTUNE

HER DIVORCE from Reid Euphrates had not only left Josie financially destitute but it had somehow managed to destroy her reputation at the same time. Once upon a time she had been a respected secondary school geography teacher, but when Reid—a journeyman singer-songwriter who had subsisted on lengthy pub tours for the last twenty years—had decided to drag her name through the mud rather than simply climbing onto his rusty old tour bus and driving away, the fallout had begun to manifest itself wherever Josie looked. She lost her job over a test scores dispute which normally would have been shrugged off, then found herself barred from both her local pub and local supermarket.

Not to worry, she had a car.

Then an article appeared in the local paper claiming she had tried to sabotage her husband's career, and suddenly her neighbours wouldn't talk to her, closing ranks around Reid, a Bristol local. She had got by thanks to a handful of loyal private students, and had thought that since she had been paying her and Reid's mortgage since day one, she might have got to keep her house.

Reid, somehow, had been able to afford an expensive lawyer who claimed he had sacrificed his income in order to be a house husband for Josie and a stay-at-home dad for Tiffany. The reality that he had spent most of their spare money on long and expensive nationwide tours during which he had done god-knows-what and left them owing enough money to promoters that Josie had needed to take a second job private tutoring to pay for, hadn't mattered when everything was said and done. Reid had suffered; she had sponged.

And now he had taken almost everything, and what he hadn't taken, she would need to sell to pay for her attempt to fight it.

The final nail in Josie's coffin had been hammered in by finding out just how Reid had managed to afford to take her legally to the cleaners in the first place.

It turned out that his new fiancée was a wealthy heiress by the name of Lady Evangeline of Suffolk. Fifty-five years old and clearly out of her mind, she had decided to finance the career of her new singer-songwriter boyfriend, and the first thing that entailed was throwing his long-suffering ex-wife into the nearest juicer and squeezing out every last drop.

'So, have you waited tables before?' asked Jonathan Able of Pebbles Fine Wine and Dining from his seat across the table, looking up from the clipboard Josie assumed held a copy of her resume and peering over the top of a vase of dried flowers.

'I helped out at a friend's wedding once,' Josie said. 'I didn't drop anything.'

'I should hope not. How are you at working under pressure?'

'I was a secondary school teacher. Pressure was my middle name.'

'It says Flora on here.'

'I didn't mean literally.'

'I see.' Jonathan squinted at the clipboard. 'There's no related reference. Was it a job you were fired from?'

'I took an offered redundancy,' Josie said, forcing a smile.

Jonathan looked up and smiled, the first time Josie had seen any genuine emotion since the interview had started. 'That's what we call it, too,' he said. 'So, no experience, and no references.'

'There's one from my university.'

'Yes, but it's more than twenty years old. The person who wrote it could quite literally be dead.'

'So?'

'Have you experienced any changes in your life over the last … generation?'

'Yes, a few things.'

'So therefore, it's no longer relevant.'

'But—'

Jonathan tapped the clipboard with his pen. 'So, no experience, no references … I suppose we could consider you for an unpaid internship, just until you learn the ropes.' He looked up and grinned. 'Would that work?'

'You want me to wait tables for free until you're satisfied that I can carry a plate of food from one corner of a room to another without perhaps managing to throw it up in the air?'

'Mrs. Roberts, if you have so little respect for the catering industry, why are you applying for a job at my restaurant?'

'Because I'm desperate?'

'Mrs. Roberts, waiting tables is so much more than

carrying plates of food from, as you say, one corner of a room to another. Good waiters are … artists.'

'I can believe that, at eleven-fifty an hour.'

Jonathan grimaced and stood up. 'Well, thank you for coming, Mrs. Roberts. I wish you luck in your continued search for employment. Should you wish to take me up on that offer of an unpaid internship, please do not hesitate to contact me.'

Josie could only sigh as Jonathan turned and walked away towards the kitchens.

'It's Ms. Roberts,' she said, shoulders slumping.

'So you're actually thinking about working for some backstreet soup kitchen for free?' Hilda said. 'Are you out of your mind? I wish a plague of Japanese knotweed on that place.'

'I've been to three job interviews this week. One told me I was too old to start a career in data entry. The second one said I wasn't tall enough to clip the tops of park hedges and that they couldn't afford the additional insurance required for me to use a stepladder. The third wanted me to wait tables for free. I'm desperate, Hilda.'

'How desperate?'

'Well, I'm not quite ready for begging outside the bus station, but give it another week and ask again.'

'If you were a tree, what kind of tree would you be?'

'Huh?'

'Just answer the question.'

Josie frowned. She reached for a cup of coffee she had just made, then took a step backwards as a spider rushed out from under the fridge and raced across the floor. The coffee sloshed; only dipping her face to take the little brown wave in the face stopped it going down the front of her dress.

'Ah, I'm an oak,' she said, wiping coffee off the end of her nose with a hem of her sleeve.

'Why?'

'I'm old.'

'Says you, talking to the woman drawing her pension. Why else?'

Josie smiled. 'I like to think I'm tough. Hard to cut down. And I would make a decent table, or at least a doorstop.'

'Resilient, that's good. Stands up in a strong wind. Doesn't run away.'

'What most trees do?'

'I've moved beyond the tree analogy now. Listen, I might have something, but I don't think it'll be easy, and you'll have to move out of Bristol.'

'Where to?'

'Down here, to where I live.'

'To Porth Melynos? You want me to come down and live in your little coastal town where rental costs are probably more than my yearly salary?'

'Technically a can of beans costs more than your current salary.'

'I take the point, but even so.'

'Look, it's not that bad. And not right in the town, but nearby. I'd offer to let you stay at my place but part of the job is that you have to live on-site. It would be rent free, too.'

'This is for a job? What is it, live-in housekeeper?'

'I'll get to the details in a moment. I have a friend who owns a place down here, just up the valley a little ways. The thing is, my friend makes me look like a freshly budding flower, and he'll take some convincing, but I can slip something herbal into his tea.' Hilda chuckled. 'The truth is, it would be lovely to have you a little nearer for the summer. And wouldn't it be nice for you to put all your troubles behind you? You could even bring Tiffany if she wants to come.'

'Tiffany? I don't know—'

'Didn't you say she's finishing up at university in a couple of months? Do you have room for her there?'

Josie looked around the flat. The truth was, she was terrified of Tiffany seeing the hellhole she now called home, to the point where she had planned to encourage her daughter to stay in London. One look at this place with its spiders, dead mice, mould, doors that didn't shut properly, ripped wallpaper, spiders, grout-covered tiles, cracked windows, and yet more spiders, and she would run off to her father, never to return.

'I suppose I could ask her. I don't know what her plans are yet. So … what is this job you said you might have?'

'Do you trust me?'

'Well, I suppose with everyone in my life except for you having either pushed me away or taken my ex-husband's side in everything, that would be a yes.'

'Good. I'll make a phone call. It won't be easy to convince my friend because it's not really a job he's aware that he has available, but before I even try, I want you to promise that you'll take up the offer if it comes.'

'Can't you just tell me what it is?'

'I don't want you to form a judgement in advance. Every challenge should be met with an open mind, rather than a preformed disposition.'

'Not even a hint?'

'Nope. Just trust me.'

3

REDUCED TO SCRAPS

'I WAS REALLY HOPING to get three hundred.'

The rotund bearded man with the glass eye sighed. 'I understand your situation,' he said, in a private school accent that defied the horror of his appearance. 'But I need a car for my ill mother. You know, it wouldn't be just that you were doing me a deal, you would be potentially adding a couple of years to someone's life. Wouldn't that make you feel like you had some kind of purpose?'

Josie gave the man a resigned smile. 'All right. Two-fifty.'

'Could you not just go to two-twenty?' He winced. 'I just felt a twinge in my hip, and remembered that I need to get a replacement.'

'Come on, they're free on the NHS.'

'Yeah, but the extra money could be spent on installing bars in my toilet, or go towards a stairlift. Wouldn't that make you feel proud?'

Josie rolled her eyes. 'All right. Two-twenty.'

'Do you think you could go down to a clean two-hundred?'

'No!'

~

IN THE END, Josie walked away from her beloved Volvo with two hundred and twenty in used banknotes. With a jovial grin, the man had offered her a lift to the bus stop, but Josie refused, walking there herself with her head down, clutching in one hand the thank-you letter from a student which she had managed to find in the pocket behind the driver's seat. On the way, she had deposited all but ten pounds into her bank account, a day before the lawyer's payment was due to go out by direct debit, essentially completing the clean-up job that Reid had begun when he had decided to finalise their divorce.

Still, once the house was sold, she would at least have some money. The dust of her humiliating divorce hadn't yet settled and he was already causing her trouble, hassling her by email about house prices, wanting a quick sale, wanting to reduce the asking price to something that would leave Josie with little more than a handful of spare change. Enough to replace her car, maybe take a holiday, but without any chance of ever getting back on the property ladder.

To celebrate cutting off another limb of her former life—and because the gas burner in the flat's kitchen made a worrying hissing noise—she bought fish 'n' chips on the way home. Then, because she really didn't want to sit in the flat on the threadbare sofa that may or may not house a mouse colony, staring at the wall with the last wreckage of her life in boxes around her, she took her package of food to a little park on the corner. There, she sat on a bench in front of a small pond, where a handful of ducks glided gently around a half-submerged sofa someone had thrown in, leaving it sticking out of the water at an angle like a sinking orange ocean liner. As she watched a duck hop from one armrest into the water, Josie wondered about pulling it out; after all, that part of it she could see was in better repair than the sofa in her flat.

By the time she had unwrapped the food, a biting wind had got up, making each chip cold before she could get it into her mouth. An old woman pushing a shopping cart filled with plastic bottles offered her a five-pound note to get herself something warm to drink.

'If you go to the offy on the corner of Williams Road, tell them Old Marge sent you,' she said with a gap-toothed smile. 'They might throw in a free bar of chocky with a bottle of the good stuff.'

Josie actually hesitated a moment before declining with thanks.

At least Tiffany should be graduating soon, she thought, munching solemnly on a piece of oily fish as Old Marge pushed her trolley away down the path. *It might have all fallen apart, but at least we got our daughter an education.*

She was going to be a doctor. Of everything that had happened in her life, that her daughter was going to be a doctor made her truly proud. Tiffany had passed all her exams, and now just had to complete a period of residency to be fully qualified. She was due to start in September, and only had to choose where she would spend her residency period. Tiffany had been talking about London, and while Josie agreed in principle, she had been hoping for Bristol or Bath, somewhere a little closer.

A piece of old newspaper billowed across the park and wrapped itself around her leg. Josie plucked it off, about to screw it up before tossing it into a nearby little bin, but a large picture near the top made her pause long enough to read the headline:

Bristol-based singer-songwriter Reid Euphrates announces nationwide tour

On the back of a viral video, popular local musician finally makes good

The picture of her smugly grinning ex made her stomach churn. She recognised the picture; it had been taken at a free charity concert about ten years ago, one for which Reid had quit his part-time job in order to rehearse, further squeezing their finances, and for which he had been paid approximately nothing.

The article went on to detail how an old song off one of her ex-husband's many Josie-funded, close-to-zero selling albums had become a viral hit on a social media website, and as a result was sitting at number two on the national music charts. Fourteen of his other songs had jumped up into the Top 40, and he was being touted as Bristol's answer to Ed Sheeran. The sudden change in fortune was estimated to be worth roughly half a million pounds.

Josie stuffed another cold chip into her mouth, chewing it like a dumb, stupid cow waiting in line for the abattoir. The newspaper was dated a week ago, one day after their divorce had been finalised, and Josie had been ordered to hand over her life savings as 'compensation for loss of earnings during the period of marriage.'

Now Reid was on his way to being a millionaire.

And just because there was always something else that could go wrong, one more arrow to land, one more rock to be thrown, the final line felt like someone swinging a big left hook to put Josie down for the count:

Just recently, Reid announced his engagement to wealthy heiress Lady Evangeline of Suffolk.

Lady Evangeline Euphrates-Barnacle.

At least Josie found herself with a reason to smile. She leant back, staring up at the sky in complete and utter defeat, then wincing as a raindrop hit her flush on the eyeball. As she blinked it away, her phone beeped in her pocket. Hoping it was good news from Hilda, she pulled it out and opened the message.

Mum … I've got something to tell you, and I'm sorry but you won't like it. I've decided not to take up the residency this year. Dad's asked me to be his manager. Isn't it great that he's suddenly getting success, after trying so hard for so long?

Josie couldn't find the energy to reply. Old Marge was on her way back, pushing her trolley, humming to herself.

'Is that offer still open?' Josie said, as the old woman reached her, bottles rattling in the trolley.

Old Marge grinned and held out a fiver. 'Don't forget to give them my name,' she said.

4

A JOURNEY INTO THE UNKNOWN

'How much of the brandy did you drink?' Hilda asked, unable to hide a chuckle.

'About half a glass. God, it was horrible. I tried putting some in a cup of tea, but that just ruined the tea. I don't think I'm designed for drowning my sorrows with alcohol. I did eat a whole packet of chocolate biscuits, though.'

'Well, that's something at least. So, your life is a mess. Always best to put a positive spin on these things. Just think about it like a jigsaw puzzle. Now you can start putting the pieces back together.'

'It's more like a broken pane of glass.'

'Well, you'd better go buy a tube of glue then, hadn't you?'

'I don't have any more money.'

'It's lucky for you that metaphorical glue is free. Do you have enough for a train ticket?'

'It depends how many stops I need to go. I have about fifteen pounds to my name.'

'Well, the good news is that my friend said yes about

the job. If you can't afford a train ticket, you'll have to hitchhike.'

'Are you serious?'

'Sometimes a bit of adversity is good for you. It makes you stronger. Did I ever tell you about the time I was in Greenland and got charged by a polar bear?'

'No?'

'That's because it didn't happen. But if it had, it would have made a great analogy.' Hilda chuckled. 'Just get down to Porth Melynos as soon as you can. Everything's going to be fine.'

'How can you be so sure?'

'Just trust me.'

'If I had a penny for every time you said that, I'd have been able to pay off my lawyer without selling my car.'

'And if I had a sapling for every time I needed to say it, I could have planted a whole forest.'

JOSIE'S COUSIN had been happy enough to give her a very reasonable rate for the two weeks she was living at the flat in Knowle, even though, as she stood with her suitcase by the bus stop, Josie couldn't help but feel like the two weeks of cleaning, fixing and tidying that she had done to make the place vaguely liveable deserved some recompense in return. As it was, though, with the majority of her remaining stuff placed into a cheap long-term storage facility, she felt lighter and airier than at any time in her life since leaving home for university more than twenty-five years ago. With just a few changes of clothes, some toiletries and a few personal items, she couldn't help feeling like she was jetting off into the unknown, even if Porth

Melynos, a tiny fishing village on the English Channel, was hardly Timbuktu.

Still, one step at a time.

She caught the train from Bristol Temple Meads to Exeter, where she changed to the Brentwell line. On the little two-carriage train she was almost alone as they bumped gently through the countryside, stopping in pretty villages with quaint names like Willow River, Olive Hill and Birch Grove. Eventually, the rolling fields gave way to views of Dartmoor to the west, the train meandering through a series of narrow valleys and stands of woodland, between which she caught a view of Plymouth to the south and the English Channel beyond as they passed around the northern edge of the city. Then they were out into the countryside again, the train crossing a bridge over the Tamar River back into Cornwall, and eventually coming to a final stop at a small countryside station called Porth Melynos Central.

As Josie climbed down from the train and walked to the end of the platform, she struggled to see what they were central to, with hedgerows all around, and only a single road leading away from a small car park. Only one other person had gotten off, and they were quickly whisked away by waiting family, leaving Josie standing alone with only the train conductor for company.

Sunset wasn't for a couple of hours until just after eight o'clock, but clouds had rolled in, threatening rain, bringing with them a bitter chill to the air that made Josie wish she'd brought a thicker coat. She pulled out her phone to call Hilda, only to find her battery had run out. Instead, she turned to look for the conductor to ask about buses, only to see the train slowly chugging out of the station, leaving her alone.

With no waiting room, no phone, and only a toilet with

an OUT OF ORDER sign on the door, Josie started to panic. Out past an unmanned ticket gate she found a bus timetable, but a connecting shuttle bus to Porth Melynos didn't start running until May. Reluctant to wait at the station for another week, she pulled her suitcase off the kerb and started walking up the road, wondering how long it would take. She hadn't seen a single sign or map, and when she climbed up on to a gate to look for the sea, all she could see were more fields.

The air did have a distinct saltiness to it, however, so perhaps if she walked in the direction of the smell? She was standing on tiptoes, sniffing at the air, when the roar of a motorcycle engine made her turn.

A sleek black motorcycle with a sidecar came roaring up the road and into the car park, its diminutive rider hunched over the handlebars, eyes hidden behind aviator goggles. Apart from a flame on the back of the helmet, the rider's attire—jacket, trousers and gloves, were all black leather.

Josie stared as the bike made a sharp turn and came back around to pull up alongside her. The rider killed the engine, then climbed off. The helmet and goggles came off, and Hilda, barely five-feet tall, hair a mess of grey curls but with a mischievous twinkle in her eyes, opened her leather-clad arms to welcome Josie with a powerful hug.

'Oh, my wonder, you made it,' she said, kissing Josie on both cheeks, her grip surprisingly strong for someone so small. 'I was sure you'd bottle it, but here you are.'

'Give me a little credit. Plus, you really should have seen the flat. I've seen the underside of bridges that are more comfortable. Not to mention … well….'

Josie wiped a tear out of her eye. Hilda huffed, then reached up and tapped her in the centre of the forehead with one forefinger.

'Josie, don't let it start. Once you start letting those thoughts have their way, you'll be stuck with them. You're here now.' She opened her hands, holding the pose for a few seconds like a mannequin at the entrance to a garden centre. 'Fresh start and all that?'

'That's right. Honestly, it's better this way.'

Hilda lifted an eyebrow that had been painted on with black eyeliner. 'Your optimism is definitely a plus. Ho, hum. You're going to need it.'

'Are you going to tell me what's going on? Like, I appreciate that it couldn't possibly be worse than what I've been dealing with, but you know, some secrets are better once revealed.'

'Ah, yes, all in good time. First let's get you down to the village before it rains. We'll grab some fish 'n' chips then have a good old chit-chat.'

'And then you'll tell me what you've invited me down here to do?'

'Yes, yes. In good time. What is it I always say to you?'

'Trust me?'

Hilda clicked gnarled old fingers together. 'Bingo. You win … one point.'

5
A DAUNTING CHALLENGE

The sun was low over the hills to the west as they negotiated a spaghetti-like series of narrow country roads, few with any signposts, many going apparently nowhere.

'Locals call it the Tangle,' Hilda shouted over the rattle of the motorbike engine, as Josie, wearing a crash helmet for the first time in her life, and partially crushed by the suitcase squeezed into the footwell in front of her, tried not to fall out as they swung around blind corners, Hilda cackling with glee every time they went wide enough to brush the opposite hedge. 'Some years ago, a bunch of local idiots pulled up most of the signs for an April Fool's joke. They hid them in a skip belonging to a local builder who was renovating a house in the village. The skip got taken away, the signs lost, and the council decided to spite the local people by not replacing them.'

'Is that a true story, or is it true like the polar bear one?' Josie shouted.

'Oh, my wonder, you know me so well,' Hilda shouted back. 'Don't worry, we're nearly there.'

A few minutes later, they came over a rise, and the V of

the English Channel appeared up ahead. The road began to steepen into a valley, and they passed a sign that read:

Porth Melynos
Welcome to Sunset Harbour

The sunset, as far as Josie could tell, would happen way over to the west, with the village facing due south. Too afraid of death on the winding lanes to query it, Hilda appeared to read her mind.

'Porth Melynos is Cornish,' she shouted by way of explanation. 'It literally translates as something like Port Yellow Night, but that's not going to look good on tourist brochures, is it?'

Josie started to shake her head, but that just make her feel queasy, so instead she nodded. Thankfully, after a couple of sharp switchbacks through shadowy corners lined by towering trees, the road both straightened and flattened, and a quaint fishing village cramped into a narrow valley appeared in front of them. Hilda slowed down, and Josie's queasiness eased just enough for her to enjoy the pretty stonewalled houses with their slate roofs, cobblestone alleyways leading to a promenade alongside a river, arched stone bridges, circular, ship-like attic windows, and pretty tourist shops and restaurants as they chugged past. She saw a handful of tea shops, confectionary shops, art galleries, and a small village museum with a pile of old sea buoys stacked outside. A pub a short distance back from a breakwater looked inviting, the triangle of grey-green sand that was the village's best attempt at a beach a little less so.

On the corner, next to a launderette, was a small fish 'n' chips shop. Hilda pulled in to a tiny parking area, then jumped off the bike, leaving the engine running. She jogged into the shop before Josie could unstrap herself and move her case enough to get out. She had just managed to get one foot onto the ground when Hilda reappeared, a bag of food in her arms. She passed it to Josie, almost pushing her back into the sidecar.

'Off we go again,' she said.

The road bumped over a humpbacked bridge and then Hilda was powering them up a steep hill leading out of the valley on the other side. They passed lines of houses built into the hillside, gardens so steep Josie could imagine the owners descending to their vegetable gardens on ropes.

At the top of the hill, they reached a pretty farm gate painted in a variety of bright colours. Beyond it was a gravel driveway leading to a two-storey house with views over the valley. Around it stood several greenhouses.

'My place,' Hilda said. 'I'd invite you in for tea, but we're pressed for time, and it would be better to eat on location.'

Josie didn't get a chance to ask what she meant. They sped through a few residential streets, then came to a stop at a closed gate just outside the village. A sign beside the entrance was hidden in the weeds, and the only word Josie could read was 'ark'.

Hilda climbed off the bike, opened the gate, then drove them through without closing it again. They bumped down a rocky, potholed lane which curved between hedgerows into a valley. Hilda finally came to a stop in a wooded grove, swaying oaks and sycamores towering overhead. Through the trees on either side of the valley stood several wooden cabins, half buried in the undergrowth. A trickling stream ran down the middle, cutting around the outside of a flat but overgrown area the size of a tennis court. Further down the valley, the trees thinned out, suggesting that the valley opened out onto the cliffs.

Hilda killed the bike's engine, then pulled off her

helmet and hung it from the handlebars. She turned to Josie and spread her arms.

'Ta da! Your adventure begins.'

Josie pulled off her helmet and set it down in the sidecar's seat as she climbed out, stretching out her stiff legs and rubbing a shoulder sore from being bumped by her suitcase on each corner.

'You're going to abandon me in the forest? Do I have to find my way out to survive? That's easy, I can just walk back up that road there.'

She nodded at the way they had come, but Hilda was shaking her head. 'No, this is your new challenge. It's rustic, I'll admit … but surely it's better than wallowing in the memories of your old life? I thought you needed a challenge to get you out of the doldrums, something to take your mind off things.' She clapped her gloved hands together. 'Nothing like a bit of hardship and some physical labour—'

'What do you mean?'

'Look at you, with your paper soft hands. You need to get down in the dirt, get some soil under those fingernails.'

'I like being clean.'

Hilda just chuckled. 'Right, let's eat these chips, before Nat turns up.'

'Nat?'

'My friend. He said he'll be here. Don't worry. He's Cornish. They do things "dreckly."'

'What does that mean?'

'It means when they feel like it. Don't worry, he'll smell the chips. He won't be long.'

They leant against the sidecar as they ate. As Hilda talked incessantly about all manner of things, the classic BMW R60 motorbike she had recently bought, a new species of rose she was working on, her plans to build a new sun-lounge room extension onto her house, Josie tried to pick up on her friend's positivity. She forced a smile, happy for Hilda, but unable to shake the black clouds that had followed her down from Bristol.

Suddenly, the snapping of a twig made her turn. Something was shuffling through the trees, bent low, leaning on a gnarled wooden staff which tapped against overhanging tree branches as the figure passed. It's course apparently random, as it made a switchback turn down the hill Josie realised it was following a meandering, overgrown path.

'Ah, here he is,' Hilda cried, clapping her hands together. 'Nat! Over here! Can't keep a Cornishman from his chips.'

The figure reached the bottom of the path and shuffled out into the clearing, the weeds parting around him. Josie could only stare in both wonder and horror. The figure was surely a man, but with more grey hair and stomach-length beard than face. Apart from a hooked nose that resembled the knot of a tree branch, the only part of him that might have been visible was his eyes, had they not been covered by a pair of incongruous black plastic sunglasses.

Nat's clothing was no more unusual than what was visible of his face. He wore a mixture of linen and sacking, with the shredded remains of a dark green woollen jumper in there too. Ragged cargo trousers covered his legs, and lumpy toes poked out from a pair of plastic sandals that looked even older than him. A signet ring glittered on the hand that gripped the staff.

'Nat, good to see you again!' Hilda exclaimed, jogging over to give the post-apocalyptic version of Father Christmas a warm hug. She took his arm and led him over to the motorcycle, steering him in a way which explained his reason for the sunglasses despite the gloominess of the forest: Nat was quite blind.

'This is Josie Roberts, the friend I was telling you about,' Hilda said.

'Maid,' Nat said, sticking out a hand which Josie felt obliged to reach for and give a quick shake. It felt like a piece of driftwood, hard and lumpy, yet simultaneously smooth and sun-warmed. Up close, the old man smelled of the sea, salty and slightly musty, like seaweed sun-dried over pebbles.

'Nice to meet you,' Josie said.

'And you, maid,' Nat said. 'Nathaniel Blackthorne. But Nat works.' He grinned, gold and silver capped teeth glinting. 'The maid here says you're looking for a project.'

'Ah, I….' Standing beside Nat, Hilda gave Josie a thumbs up, then a surreptitious nod towards Nat which suggested he was some kind of deity to be respected. 'I … found myself between jobs. Anything you have would be a great help.'

'Twas nervous about giving the old girl a go,' Nat said, still shaking Josie's hand. He glanced around, leaving Josie unsure whether the 'old girl' was herself, Hilda, or some other, perhaps abstract concept. 'Been a while, after all. Folks've moved on. The maid here convinced me, so if you want the challenge, it's yours. Me, though, I ain't one to do nothing by halves. You're all in, or all out, so to speak. Since you'll be doing all the work, you can have two-thirds.' He grinned again. 'I'll take me third as silent overlord.'

'Uh, sure.'

'Then welcome.'

'Thanks. Just to clarify … where exactly are we?'

Nat let go of her hands and stumbled around in a circle, hands out like a shaman calling for rain. 'Maid, you be the new manager of Porth Melynos Caravan and Camping Park.'

6
UNWELCOME RESIDENTS

'But there's nothing there,' Josie said, a glass of wine in one hand as she gestured to Hilda with the other. Through the pub window, a few lights shone from the fishing boats tied up in the small harbour. The last of the sun left an orange swathe across the eastern cliffside that gradually gave way to shadow. 'It's just a forest with a few abandoned cabins in it. How long did you say since it last opened?'

Hilda grinned. 'It closed at the end of the summer of 1989. So that's what, thirty-five years? Come on, Josie, it'll be fun. You've got nothing to lose.'

'Technically you're right, but … I mean, I don't know the first thing about running a campsite.'

'You'll figure it out. You have a month or so to get ready for the season. That should be plenty of time.'

'To literally build a campsite from the ground up!'

'You're overreacting. It's just camping. All you need to do is cut the grass and clear the spiders out of the toilet block. Nat's had your cabin reconnected to gas and electric, and the park's plumbing is good. And all the licences and regulations are up to date because he forgot to cancel everything after his father closed the campsite. So you're not going to get inspectors or council types trying to shut you down.'

'Cut the grass,' Josie said, rubbing her eyes. 'Just cut the grass.'

'I've got a scythe you can use. Just in case things are bit thick for a petrol strimmer. Don't you remember teaching Tiffany to walk?'

'She bounced off everything in sight.'

'And now's she's nearly qualified as a doctor. You must have done something right. If you can raise a child into a doctor, you can raise a campsite out of the forest.'

Josie gulped down the last of her wine, then covered her mouth with a hand as she started to cough. She wanted to tell Hilda about Tiffany, but it was one humiliation too great. She was yet to respond to her daughter's message. She just didn't know what to say to convey the witch's cauldron of emotions the message had stirred up.

'Baby steps,' Hilda said. 'Believe me, this will be good for you. I'm there to help, and Nat said he's available if you have any questions. Look, if you get through this, just think how proud you'll feel.'

The background music playing gently in the pub suddenly changed, and Josie lurched to her feet, grabbing the back of the chair for support as her spinning vision threatened to make her keel over.

'Are you all right?'

'I need some air. This song … I can't listen to this song.'

'*I tried my best because she took the rest; when I stood my ground, she burnt my house down—*'

Hilda had been swaying from side to side, tapping her

hand on the table as she mouthed along to the lyrics. 'Oh, my wonder, this isn't it, is it? Reid's song?'

Josie didn't wait to reply. She ran out of the pub and across the street to the harbourside wall. Peering down at the black water gushing through the gloomy river channel, she resisted the urge to jump in. Instead, she kicked at a nearby bollard, serving only to hurt her foot.

She was still hopping up and down when Hilda, leaning on a stick, came outside and wandered over.

'Are you all right?'

'Absolutely not. My entire life is a total and utter shambles. You know, he wrote that song while we were married. He told me it was a "hypothetical situation". Do you know how many people have asked if I really burnt down his house?'

'Go on, enlighten me. How many?'

Josie tried to count. There had been the woman at the post office, but she'd been fluttering her eyelashes at Reid for years. Then there had been….

'One,' she said with a resigned sigh. 'People don't even know he was married.'

'Perhaps that's for the best?' Hilda said, patting her on the back. 'Now, are you going to be sick? For if not, it's a little chilly, isn't it? Perhaps we should go back inside and order something to warm us up.'

'Brandy?'

'I was thinking more of hot chocolate, but you do what you need to do.'

JOSIE WOKE on her first morning in Porth Melynos Caravan and Camping Park with a mild hangover. As she rolled over on the hard wooden pallet that served as her bed, peering up at the cabin's slat roof, through a narrow gap between two of which the sunlight glittered through the trees, she thought that at least she wasn't in hell, otherwise she might be a bit warmer.

She pulled back the blankets Hilda had lent her and sat up. The room swayed, although mostly with her lack of confidence and self-belief. She was a failure. Her life was a failure. Everything was a total disaster.

Baby steps, Hilda had said. What was step number one?

Josie forced a smile.

Of course.

Coffee.

The cabin, three connecting rooms made entirely of pieces of varnished pine nailed together, at least had a semblance of a kitchen, a small worktop, a gas hob and a microwave. While the electric and gas worked as Hilda had promised, the sink was filled with dead flies floating in a gunky green residue, reminding Josie that she had tried the long-unused taps last night. Now, much to her relief, the water ran clean, even if it did have a slightly grainy taste.

She drank two large glasses of water, then found some coffee—another donation from Hilda—and heated some water over the hob. Some powdered milk took away a little of the bitterness, but she would need a fridge for some real milk if she was somehow going to make this work.

Carrying her coffee, she slipped on a pair of sandals and went outside. Stacked concrete blocks lifted the cabin off the ground, and a pile of stones and earth that had settled over the years into a solid pile made for an awkward set of steps. At the bottom, an overgrown path led down through the trees into the main camping area.

Outside, surrounded by trees, a sense of peace fell over Josie. For the first time in a while she felt disconnected from all her troubles. As long as she stayed here in this valley, she was safe. Down here no one could get to her, take away her dignity, humiliate her … nor contact her by phone, as there was zero reception unless you walked up the lane to the gate on the coastal road. Here, she was cut off from the world.

How difficult could it possibly be to open and run a campsite? Even if the caravans were beyond use, all she needed to provide for campers was a bit of open space to put up their tents. There was a toilet block, of course, which Nathaniel claimed still had running water and just needed a decent clean, 'Plus a few saplings grown up through the tiles need hacking down,' so all she really needed was to cut a path down to the beach supposedly at the bottom of the valley, then perhaps clear the weeds off the sign up on the road, so campers would know where to come.

Easy.

Was it?

She walked a little way down the path to what had once been the campsite's parking area. Weeds came up to her knees, and a tree had fallen across the road on the way in, so long ago that saplings had been to grow up around it, creating a natural screen of vegetation.

She walked a little further. The trees opened out a little and she found herself facing a padlocked barn, partly reclaimed by the forest, with one tree growing in through a side window and out through a hole in the roof. She had no key for the padlock, but as she peered through a gap in the boards of the door, she saw the outline of what looked like ping pong and pool tables, plus an indoor children's play area.

There was more here than she had thought, it seemed. Walking a little further, she came across a couple of overgrown buildings, one which might have been a shop, another that looked like a camping rental place. And then a little further on, she found some kind of tower, a tall cone so choked in weeds and vines that the only indication it was man-made came from a few silver glints through the upper vine leaves. Taller than a two-storey house, she wondered if it was some kind of lookout tower.

Thinking about cutting her way in later, she headed on. The trees began to thin out, and she caught glimpses of a grassy clearing up ahead. Here, the sea sounded close. She pushed her way through, thinking she was close to the beach.

Voices drifted through the trees, making Josie halt in her tracks. No, not voices, chanting. Voices rose and fell, feeding off each other, some baritone, others falsetto, creating an awkward discordance that made Josie wince.

Only a couple of trees separated her from the clearing. She looked down at her feet and realised she was walking on a well-trodden path. One more step and she broke through the tree line just as the grass in front of her seemed to move.

Josie let out a gasp of fright as the vegetation lifted up and turned, revealing the faces of four people wearing bizarre costumes made out of woven grass, leaves and tree branches. She started to back away but found a tree at her back.

'Don't hurt me!' she cried, even as the group let out a howl that lay somewhere between fear and threat, as though it had been years since they had been faced with such a situation and were unsure how to react. Then, backed up against the cliff edge, they looked around at each other. Beards waved, long, unkempt hair swayed in the wind, and clothing Josie now realised was comprised of ancient rags repaired by whatever they could find in the forest, rustled. Then, with a low 'coo' that indicated a decision, they turned and rushed at Josie as one.

She stumbled backwards, trying to get away, but as she twisted, she caught her foot on a rock protruding out of the soil and fell flat on her face, scratching her cheek on a thorny bush and catching her forehead with a glancing blow against a sapling's trunk that had just enough flexibility not to knock her out.

By the time she had recovered herself, the group had vanished. As she sat up, leaning back against the base of the tree, she looked around, wondering what was going on. Perhaps she had been knocked out, as the ground had disappeared, and as she peered back into the gloom below the trees, she couldn't catch any sight of them. Rubbing her head as she looked across the clearing, she recognised the rotted remains of a picnic bench standing close to the cliff edge, so she climbed stiffly to her feet, brushed herself down, and went to take a look.

The bench was still intact, but the seats had rotted away. In their place, four metal-framed deckchairs had been arranged in a semi-circle, frames rusty, canvas seats sun-faded and frayed, repaired with twigs and baler twine. Beyond the bench, the ground dropped away, a steep grassy slope with a well-trodden path meandering back and forth. Halfway down to a crescent-shaped beach it intersected with another path following the line of the cliff. This had to be the southwest coast path, for it looked well-used. Where the path down from the clearing intersected it, there was a barbed wire fence and a wooden sign she couldn't read from this distance. Beyond it, the downward path continued, meandering down to the shore.

She had never been much of a beach person, not liking the feel of sand on her toes or the saltiness of seawater in her hair. As she stared at the little beach, however, she felt a sudden sense of longing. On the right, a steep, curving jut of rock wrapped around it like a protective arm. Cragged and treacherous, the coast path rose up out of the valley then dropped over the headland's shoulder, not attempting to make it out to the narrow end. Another clearing stood there, distant benches the size of doll's house toys facing out to the sea. To her left, the cove was a little more open, the cliff a fat lump of shale rock with a stand of gnarled, misshapen trees on top. Together, the two cliffs held the tiny cove like a child in its parents' arms, safe and protected. Small breakers lapped at a semi-circle of grey sand backed by a foreshore of lumpy slate rocks. In the water, three small rock stacks jutted out, one just offshore, two others at diagonals to the right and left, a little larger, a little further out.

As Josie stared, letting her eyes relax and her vision blur, she couldn't help but think it looked like the smiling face of a man, the rocks the eyes and nose, the headlands large ears or even sideburns, the grey beach a smile. As a small wave broke over the shore, the whitewater resembled a bushy moustache.

Josie leant back against the bench, smiling to herself, the sun high overhead warming her skin. While it would never stand up against some paradisical tropical island, it was a rugged little gem of a place, and while she still didn't have any confidence in herself, the view at least was enough to draw her out of her problems for a few moments.

Something rustled against her ankle, tickling the strip of skin above her shoes. She reached down and picked it up.

An empty wrapper, the design on the side reading Suncrust Pasties.

Josie frowned. She turned back to the trees, wondering

where the strange people had gone, then to her horror realised they were still there, watching her.

Not on the ground, however, but high up in the branches of the trees, peering out from among the leaves, like a group of squirrels waiting for the fox to leave so that their foraging could resume.

As she stared at them, her neck prickling at the thought that they had been watching her during a moment she had thought she was alone, a sudden sound rose out of the trees, something that at first sounded like a strange animal cry, before Josie realised was the name of a man chanted over and over again:

'Mike! Mike, Mike! Mike, Mike, *Mike!*'

7

ROBINSON

HILDA LIFTED her teacup to her lips and took a little sip. Josie, with a strong black coffee, stared past her friend, through the café window at the sweeping view of Porth Melynos in the valley below. On another day she might have marvelled at the quaint harbour with its narrow streets of pretty stonewalled houses, but now all she could think about was the terror she had felt back at the campsite after finding the people living in the trees.

'I can't go back there,' she said, hands shaking as she tried to grip her coffee. 'It was like … some kind of horror film. I could see their treehouses in there, like all rope bridges and balconies, like that Ewok village in *Star Wars*.'

'*The Return of the Jedi*, dear,' Hilda said. 'The Ewoks didn't appear until the third film.'

'I don't care. It was terrifying. I saw four of them. I can't go back there, not knowing they're so close. Like, their clothes were all make of sticks.'

'Perhaps we could have a word with Nat, see what he says.'

'I need to go back and get my stuff, then I'm leaving.'

A look of horror passed across Hilda's face, and she reached across the table to pat Josie's hand. 'Please, don't be so hasty. You have to give it time.'

'They could murder me in my bed!'

'Oh, you're overreacting. They were probably just messing around. Kids playing a game.'

'They had beards. Some of them looked older than me.'

'Well, perhaps they were actors training for a role. Who knows?'

'They were crazy forest people. And who or what is Mike? Is that a Cornish word that means lunch? I nearly killed myself running down that path, and by the time I got back here I felt like I'd climbed Everest. How steep is that coast path?'

'Nothing like a good workout in the morning,' Hilda said. 'Don't worry, you'll sort it out.'

'No, I won't. I'm leaving. I'd rather go back to that horrible dirty flat in Bristol than deal with a group of bloodthirsty weirdos who live in trees.'

'And who eat Suncrust Pasties,' Hilda said with a smile. 'They have good taste, I'll give them that. Did you know, Suncrust used to be Dirgils? Dirgils, Dirgils, fit for gerbils.' She chuckled to herself. 'We used to sing that years ago, back at school. Someone bought the company out a few years ago, renamed them Suncrust, and gave them an overhaul. Best pasties in the Southwest these days.'

'I bet they were filled with human flesh. I'm leaving before I end up in one.'

Hilda's smile dropped. 'Please, Josie. Don't give up. Do it for me.'

Josie sighed. Her instinct was telling her to get out of Porth Melynos as fast as she could, but was returning to Bristol really the best option? The gloomy, dirty flat with its spiders, no job, friends of her ex-husband seemingly in every corner?

'Will you come with me when I go to talk to Nat?' she said quietly.

Hilda smiled. 'That's my girl. Of course I will.' She gave a little chuckle. 'I doubt you'd be able to find his place on your own, anyway.'

NATHANIEL, it turned out, lived in a wood-framed cabin on the clifftop only half a mile from the caravan park, but behind a gate with a threatening sign: KEEP OUT – BULLS ABOUT. At the end of a wide, overgrown field, what was little more than a tumbledown shack occupied a grassy bowl with panoramic views out across the English Channel. Stands of gnarled trees gave it some shelter, but even on a warm day the sea wind rushed up the field with so much power that Josie and Hilda had to lean forwards to avoid being blown over as they struggled down a gravel track alongside the hedge. Josie glanced around nervously for the aforementioned bulls, but other than a few rabbits and a solitary goat sheltering by a distant hedge, the field was empty.

Nataniel's shack bore all the marks of years of wind abuse. Salt-blasted wood, faded paint. Poorly fitting windows had frayed masking tape across the glass, and several roof tiles had been replaced by pieces of plywood or black plastic sheeting.

Around the shack was a smorgasbord of sea detritus: piles of old buoys, heaps of fishing net, large plastic drums filled with abstract junk like old shoes, glass bottles, plastic containers, and huge pieces of driftwood, some that likely took a tractor to haul up from the beach. Many of these last were in the process of being carved into intricate designs. At the sight of a line of life-sized sparrows carved out of one section of sea-smoothed wood, Josie's jaw nearly hit the ground. Blind, he might be, but Nathaniel was an expert wood sculptor.

They walked up to the door, framed by a couple of hardy bushes in plant pots. Rickety and rattling in the wind, Josie doubted it would withstand a strong knock, let alone a winter storm, so she stood on the step instead and called out, 'Nathaniel? Are you in there?' Behind her, Hilda chuckled as she inspected one of the bushes, the pot scraping on a paving slab as she twisted it around.

'That's better, get a bit more sun on this side….'

'Nathaniel?' Josie called again. 'It's Josie, from the campsite. I'm here with Hilda. I wanted to ask if you know anything about a group of people living in a treehouse—well, several treehouses—on the campsite property. Nathaniel? Are you in there?'

'Hang on a minute,' came an unfamiliar voice from inside. It was deeper, smoother than Nathaniel's, the words carrying less of an accent.

The door inched open. One hinge was loose so the person inside had to lift the door a little to stop it falling off. A pair of hands appeared, working the door to half-way, then a man's face peered out.

Mid-forties, perhaps, sun-bleached unkept hair and tanned, prematurely lined skin that clearly spent too much time in the sun, the man had a kind if somewhat perplexing smile. He looked at Josie, giving a little shake of his head.

'All right? Can I help you with something?'

'Ah … I … you're not Nathaniel.'

'Oh, Robinson!' came Hilda's voice. 'You're home again?'

'Mrs. Lewisham,' the man said with a wide grin as he shifted the door back a few more inches. 'Lovely to see you again.'

He squeezed past the broken door out onto the front step, and leant past Josie to shake Hilda's hand. Josie flinched back as he came uncomfortably close, smelling of both paint and sweat, as though he hadn't washed his clothes in some time.

'This is Josie,' Hilda said, patting Josie on the arm. 'My best friend. She's from Bristol. She's just came out of a bad divorce and has come down here to recover. Your dad was good enough to give her a job as manager of your grandad's old campsite.'

Robinson frowned at Hilda, then opened his mouth in a half-smile and cocked his head. Josie tried to kick Hilda in the ankle and missed, only managing to kick the nearest plant pot instead.

'Ah, Mrs. Lewisham—'

'Hilda, please, dear.'

'Mrs…. ah Hilda … ah, is that some kind of joke?'

'Divorce is not a joke, Robinson.'

'I meant about the park. It's been closed since I was a kid. Dad has no interest in opening it up again.'

It was Hilda's turn to take an ankle swing, this time aiming at Robinson. She also missed, also hitting the poor flowerpot, which wobbled and might have overturned had Josie not squatted down to steady it. She shuffled off the step and stood on the grass beside the door, watching Robinson shaking his head and chuckling.

'That's not what your dad told me,' Hilda said.

Josie put up a hand. 'Excuse me, can we just rewind a little bit? Ah, hello. So, I'm Josie. You're Nathaniel's son, I take it?'

'That's right.'

'Is your dad here?'

'No, he's down on the beach. He'll be back sooner or later, when he finds his way up.'

'When he ... isn't he blind?'

Robinson grinned, nodding. 'Yeah. That's why it takes a while. Hates being helped, though. Typical old Cornishman. Thinks he's immortal. One day he'll just walk right off the edge of one of the cliffs and vanish into the sea.'

'So ... you don't know when he'll be back?'

'Nope. Hopefully not for a while. I've been doing a bit of painting. This place is a mess.' He grinned. 'Dad doesn't care now he can no longer see it, but I have slightly higher standards.'

'We just had a couple of questions about the camping park,' Hilda said.

'Well, if Dad really did say he wanted it reopened, I imagine you can do whatever you want. You know what Dad's like.'

'Would he mind if I chopped down a couple of trees?'

Robinson grinned. 'Probably not. Although if you do, save the wood.' He poked a thumb over his shoulder. 'This place is falling apart. Haul them up here and I'll do the rest.'

'Haul them ... right.' Josie had begun to feel dizzy. 'Okay. Maybe I'll just do that.'

Robinson lifted an eyebrow. 'Anything else? Sorry not to invite you in, but I have paint everywhere.'

'We'd better get back to work anyway,' Hilda said. 'Tell your dad we dropped by.'

'Will do.'

Robinson went back inside, lifting the door again to close it. Hilda turned to Josie, taking her arm and steering her back up the lane.

'See? No problem. You can do what you like.'

'So, I can set fire to those treehouses and throw the bodies of those tree huggers into the sea?'

Hilda chuckled. 'Oh, Josie. Don't be so dramatic. Just tell them to leave or you'll call the police.'

'I'm really not sure I can do this.'

'You can, and you will. Robinson … he's grown up, hasn't he?'

'Was he recently a child? And I mean, physically, not his personality.'

'Don't be silly. He's been away for a few years, but every time I see him, he seems to have got just a little more hunkier.'

'What? Are you serious?'

Hilda let out a giggle that made Josie cringe. 'Don't pretend you didn't notice. Did you see how I dropped that point about your divorce in there, just so he knows that you're single?'

'I'm really not interested in painter and decorators.'

'They probably earn more than singer-songwriters.'

Josie couldn't help but smile. 'Even so, I'm still not interested. Even if I did like him—which I don't—I can't even think about that kind of stuff right now. It's all too … fresh.'

'Oh, Josie, you're such a cynic.'

'I am not. I'm an optimist. That's why I'm still here instead of running for the bus stop to escape.'

'So, you've decided to stay?'

Josie let out a long sigh. 'Only until the next thing goes wrong.'

Hilda hopped up and down on one foot. 'How wonderful. Come on, let's go and get some coffee at mine. I want to show you a couple of my new rose designs. You know, a company in Japan offered me half a million for my patent on a new blue rose design I'm working on. I'm not sure whether to accept or not.'

'You even need to think about it?'

'Money isn't everything,' Hilda said.

'So, it's coffee at your cavernous, five-bedroomed house—'

'Six, dear. Five not including mine.'

'Your six-bedroomed house, and then you'll wave me goodbye as I trudge off to my dirty little cabin in the woods, where my chances of becoming a serial killer's victim are approximately five-hundred times greater?'

Hilda grinned and patted Josie on the arm. 'The greater the challenge, the greater the reward, dear.'

8

SEA CURRENTS

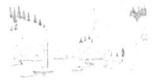

DESPITE BARRICADING the door to her shack with an old table, Josie slept poorly, waking up to incessant rain outside. As she peered out of the door, wondering whether she would find a wicker man erected in the clearing outside, she couldn't help but feel a pang of regret that Hilda had convinced her to stay.

First things first. As a teacher, making lists and keeping notes had kept her from going insane or being crushed beneath a pile of unfinished tasks. She stared out at the remains of the campsite, mentally taking stock of everything, wondering where she ought to start.

There was nothing much that could be done outside with the rain, but there were a number of cabins hidden away among the trees. She grabbed a raincoat and an umbrella and headed out. Within a few steps her shoes were caked with sloppy mud, and she could feel it getting right down into her toes. Wellington boots went on the list.

She found eight cabins, all padlocked. While vines had reclaimed a couple, through grimy windows the insides looked in relatively good order, even if the décor was a little out of date.

It was likely Nat had the padlock keys hidden away somewhere, but with no inclination to trudge up a muddy hillside to his house, she went looking around the campsite instead, wondering what else she might find. The play barn in the centre was also padlocked, but wandering about in the rain, she came across the shower and toilet block Nat had mentioned, with taps that actually worked, and to her even greater surprise, had hot water. While the drains immediately began to back up, clogged with years of mud and fallen leaves, the warm water felt good on her hands, and she even managed a smile.

'Come on, Josie,' she muttered to herself, glancing up at the tree canopy overhead as she realised that for the first time that morning the rain had actually stopped.

Things were looking up.

Near the edge of the trees, where the gravel road entered the forest, she found an old signboard lying in the hedge, its wooden legs rotted away. The surface, however, was durable plastic, and after wiping off thirty years of crusted dirt, she found herself presented with a map of the park.

To her surprise, there was a welcome cabin which doubled as a camping shop hidden behind vegetation not twenty yards away. After digging her way through ferns, brambles and vines, she peered through a grimy window to see a line of keys hung up on hooks behind a reception counter. The door itself required a regular key—which she of course didn't have—but things were still looking up.

The map threw up some other surprises, too. It turned out that the tower thing she had found was a helter-skelter, the tallest permanent structure in Cornwall, and part of a wider children's park and play area which included a section called 'Treetop Adventure Land'. Josie scowled at a cartoonish picture of several interconnected treehouses with smiling children playing among the walkways, and vowed to reclaim them.

An hour later, she found herself trudging down the path to Nathaniel's place. This time, Robinson was nowhere to be seen, but Nathaniel was outside, standing by a giant piece of driftwood, chipping away at it with a knife.

He grinned when she told him what she wanted.

'Ah, maid, I don't have coin for anything like that,' he said. 'Me's a man of simple means.'

'I can't do it all myself,' Josie said. 'I mean, I can clean, and probably figure out how to patch a few things up, but I can't do a place like that on my own. It's too big.'

'Hang on a sec.'

Nathaniel put down his knife, turned and stumbled, seemingly from memory, back to his shack. He went inside, then emerged again five minutes later.

'Here's what I've got, maid,' he said, grinning. 'This'll start 'e on right path.'

'What's that?'

'Transistor radio. You can listen to the cricket. Keep yer mind busy, free yer hands up for the task.'

'It's April.'

'Ah, start them games early these days, don't they?'

'But—'

'No need for no fancy tinternet down there, is there?'

'Internet.'

''Twas what I said. Tinternet.'

'Right.'

'And I got these for 'e.'

A gnarled old hand reached into his pocket and took out a keyring. Fingers as twisted as the driftwood he carved held up a key attached to a silver Cornish pasty.

'What does that open?'

'Barn. Inside, on left, you'll find key for the shop hanging up. All other keys inside.' He grinned, a gold tooth glinting in the sun. 'Big on me security, me.'

'But I need cleaning goods, tools. I just sold everything I owned to pay for a divorce lawyer who lost me everything.'

'Who needs money?' Nat said. 'Get a bit of barter going. Tit for tat. But if you do go up garden centre, this'll sort 'e out. Found him on the beach yesterday.'

He reached into his other pocket and held up a crumpled twenty-pound note which he handed to Josie.

'You … found that on the beach? How? I thought you were—'

Nathaniel grinned. 'Like any good wolf, I can smell the old spondoola.'

'Seriously?'

'Nah, 'twas in a bottle.'

'Really?'

'Uh huh.'

'You found a bottle washed up on the beach with a twenty-pound note in it? Was there anything else inside?'

'Yeah, message. Didn't read it. The eyes, you know.' He grinned, tapping the side of his sunglasses.

'What did you do with it?'

'Threw it back. Ain't no one gonna find it down there. Give it six months, current'll take it down Mount's Bay.'

Josie could only shake her head. 'Well, thanks.'

'Go up garden centre, give 'em that, open me a tab. Tell 'em I'll settle dreckly.'

'Right.'

'That all? Sorry lass, got to get back to work. Inspiration's like a sea current, don't you know. Catch it while it's there or you're becalmed for days.'

As he shuffled back to his sculpture, Josie turned and trudged back up the path to the road, a radio, a key and twenty pounds better off, but still with little clue how she was going to get the campsite open and running.

By the time she reached Hilda's place in order to beg for a lift up to the garden centre, she realised she had forgotten to ask Nathaniel about the people living in the treehouses. With a sigh, she wondered if twenty pounds would be enough to bribe them to go away.

HILDA WAS ONLY TOO happy to oblige, and an hour later, she dropped Josie back down at the campsite armed with several bags of cleaning materials—to Josie's surprise, the garden centre's manager had actually agreed to set a tab up for Nathaniel—a petrol strimmer on loan from Hilda, and a brand new pair of wellington boots. She had also gone so far as to buy some batteries for the transistor radio. To her surprise, she did manage to find a station airing the commentary for an cricket match abroad, but having no clue as to the rules or what any of the terminology meant, she tuned in to a radio drama station instead.

The barn padlock took a bit of wrestling with, but just as she was about to give up and go hunting for a sledgehammer, the lock turned with a rusty clunk and she was able to get inside. Again, to her surprise, the electric lights still worked, but as soon as she turned them on, half of the bulbs—likely not used for decades—blew out.

The ones that had survived, however, gave her just enough light to see as she padded up a concrete walkway that had once been covered with some kind of flooring, although little more than a few shreds now remained intact. While it might once have been blue, it was now a smeared, water-damaged green. In walled-off sections were ping pong and pool tables, an indoor play area for smaller children, and a seating area that might have once been a café, even if now all that remained was a dirty bar covered in vines that had got inside through a crack in the wall.

As she wandered from section to section, however, she stopped regarding it as essentially a ruin. Instead, she began to do something that she couldn't remember doing in a long time: dream. Many of the campsite's facilities were in decent repair, needing little more than a good clean up and a lick of paint. And while some parts revealed more of the passage of time than others, with a bit of work this campsite could be spectacular. And filled with the laughter of holidaymakers and their children, it could be a quite wonderful place indeed.

She was humming a little tune to herself as she walked back through the barn to the entrance. Just as she was coming out of the heavy gates, however, she caught sight of movement among the trees. She hurried to the edge of the barn just in time to see four figures dashing away through the forest in the direction of the treehouse village.

The squatters. Buoyed by her new aspirations, rather than feeling afraid, Josie's temper rose. It was time they got a piece of her mind. They couldn't stay here, and she wasn't going to let them.

She went back to her cabin, where she had left the strimmer and the things she had bought. Everything looked untouched, and she couldn't see anything that was missing. As she went to pick up one of her shopping bags, however, something fat and green jumped out, bounced off her chest, and hopped away into the undergrowth.

Josie patted her chest, aware she had let out a scream of fright. Only a frog, but it had been a really big one, perhaps a toad, although she wasn't sure. It had been right inside one of her bags, even though she had put it down on the steps.

The four people she had seen running had been coming from the direction of her cabin.

Had they been responsible for the frog?

She checked in her other bags, but there were no others. Perhaps it had just got in there by itself. She sighed, then sat down on the bottom step to catch her breath, her heart still thundering after the shock.

And then she saw it.

In a patch of sticky mud just to the side of the steps, the print of a human foot.

9

CLEARING OUT THE ATTIC

'I KNOW you can hear me up there,' Josie shouted, hands cupped around her mouth. 'I'm willing to be reasonable about this, but you can't stay up there, and you certainly can't cause me any trouble. I appreciate that some people like frogs, but I don't. One more trick like that and I'm calling the police.'

She waited, staring up at the undersides of the treehouses. Safe enough for children, they were only ten feet off the ground, and with a stepladder she could have climbed up, but rather than confront these people directly, she wanted to reason with them first. And in any case, what if they were dangerous? She felt it unlikely; putting a frog in her shopping was hardly an act of mass sabotage, but even so, it showed enough intent that she had to tread lightly.

'By the way,' she called up, lowering her voice a little. 'Can you please pick up your pasty wrappers? Although I applaud your choice. I had a Suncrust for lunch. Best pasty I've had in years.'

She thought she heard a murmur from inside one of

the treehouses. A wooden board creaked, but even though she waited for a couple of minutes, no further response came. With a sigh, Josie turned and trudged back through the forest to her cabin.

It was best to keep busy. It would take her mind off things—and really, if a bunch of tree-living, grass clothing-wearing hippies thought they were the biggest problem she had, they should consider a costly divorce and a daughter dropping out of medical school—and a bit of exercise was always good for a troubled mind. She tried to remember who had told her that: it was probably Hilda. Her friend had as many motivational sayings as she did botany awards.

Josie guessed it was best to start at the top and work her way down. Taking the strimmer and a couple of scythes also on loan from Hilda, she hacked away the undergrowth around the entrance, then started pulling down the vines from the camp reception and shop. As she worked, she made a mental note of what she would need—and find some way to fund; although she felt confident she could lean on Hilda for a loan if necessary—and what would require specialist skills to repair.

While she could pull down vines, cut away vegetation, hold a paintbrush and change a few lightbulbs, she couldn't repair frayed wiring or replace a broken window pane, fix a buckled roof or seal a split gas canister pipe. At some point she would have to call for outside help, but the harder she worked, the harder she wanted to work. The hours rushed past, and when she heard the rumble of Hilda's gardening van bumping down the path, she glanced at her watch and was surprised to see it was nearly seven o'clock. She had been working since before lunch with little more than a break to sip some water.

'Huh, I never knew that was there,' Hilda said,

pointing at the uncovered reception building as she climbed out of her truck. 'It looks like you're doing a great job. I just thought I'd pop down and see how you were getting on.'

Josie smiled. 'It's a work in progress,' she said. 'But it's getting there.'

'Are you ready to break for some dinner?' Hilda grinned. 'It's curry and a pint night at the pub.'

Josie frowned. 'Neither of which I thought would interest you....'

Hilda shrugged. 'Things have changed. Don't worry, we'll drive down, get a taxi back up. Just in case you're a bit worse for wear, you can stop over at mine tonight.'

'But a queen needs to be at her palace.'

'Not when it's curry and a pint night. Come on, grab something decent to wear and I'll take you over to my place for a rinse down. I think you have a bird's nest in your hair.'

Josie scrabbled at her head, but came away only with a couple of leaves. She glared at Hilda, who shrugged and gave a little smirk.

'I guess my eyes aren't what they used to be.'

THE HORSE AND BUOY INN, Porth Melynos's premier pub, was set just back from the harbour, a dramatic and beautiful stonewalled building with pleasant landscaped gardens to the side and rear. Even though late April was still a little chilly, several tables were occupied outside. Josie caught a couple of upcountry accents mixed with the gravelly ones of locals. A couple of kids played on a climbing frame at the bottom of the garden, while the smell of curry wafted out of the pub's kitchen windows.

'Not sure my ulcers will handle a phaal, so we'll likely go for a mid-to-high heat tikka,' Hilda said, rubbing her hands together as they walked up the path.

'You have ulcers?'

'Who doesn't at my age? What are you thinking of having?'

'Oh, just something mild. A korma will do.'

'Don't you want something to put some fire into your belly? You were saying about those strange people. Did you have a word with Nat?'

'I went up there but I forgot. I have to admit, I'm a little nervous about them being there.'

They pushed in through the doors and took a table by the wall. About half the tables were occupied, the food a mixture of curries and old-fashioned pub staples. A few people sat by the bar, chatting amicably over beer and wine. A fire flickered in a grate, paintings of the harbour and cliffs hung from the stone walls, and photographs of old local sports teams hung above the bar. A shelf of books stood in a corner, a stack of board games and magazines in another. Beside the fireplace was a sculpture made out of driftwood and fishing nets. At first Josie had no idea what it was supposed to be, before squinting a little and realising it was a representation of a mermaid sitting on rocks. Even once she had seen it, however, she couldn't be entirely sure.

'Is that one of Nathaniel's?' she asked Hilda as her friend scoured a laminated menu.

'Oh, yes. I think so. It's been there a while. I think he's better now that he's blind, though.' She raised a hand in the air, then suddenly let out a gasp of surprise.

'Cathy? Is that you?'

A big, boisterous woman wearing a white blouse over black trousers, with an apron adorned with a seashells pattern tied around her waist came blustering over. A shoulder-length bob of hair bounced up and down as she clapped her hands together hard enough to make half the conversation in the pub stop.

'Hil? Oh my word, Hil? Is that you?'

'Cathy!'

Hilda stood up to greet the other woman, who dwarfed her both in height and width. Cathy leant in and gave Hilda a surprisingly delicate kiss on the cheek, before clapping her hands together again. The gentle background music, which had seemed to pause, now seemed to rise again as people on the surrounding tables resumed their conversations.

'Oh my, Hil, I thought for a minute I'd been struck by a speeding pasty van when I saw you just then,' the big woman said. 'What brings you down here?'

'Just a night out with my best friend,' Hilda said, indicating Josie, who gave Cathy a shy smile. 'Cathy Ubbers, this is Josephine Roberts.'

'Nice to meet you,' Josie said, sticking out a hand which was immediately swallowed up by a huge and podgy, but surprisingly powerful, paw. Cathy gave her hand a tug hard enough to make Josie's shoulder ache, then let out a dramatic sigh.

'It's Cathy Ubbers-Benson these days. 'Me and Gav got hitched. I so wished you could have been there.'

'I was in Antarctica.'

Cathy let out a guffaw and gave Hilda a playful punch on the arm. 'Oh, you. Any excuse.' She turned to Josie. 'What brought you down here, Jose? On hols?'

'Divorce,' Josie said.

Cathy let out a hysterical laugh. 'Oh my, I can see why you two are friends. Anyway, I'd better get back to the kitchen, lol. Them curries ain't gonna cook themselves.'

'Do you work here now?' Hilda asked.

'Volunteer,' Cathy said. 'Gav's now a stay-at-home dad for the little three.' She leant down as though to whisper something, but her voice was loud enough for half the pub to hear. 'Number four's in the oven. He thought it would be nice for me to get out and about while I have the chance.'

She laughed again, slapping the table hard enough to make a basket of condiments rattle, then marched off without another word.

'She's … nice,' Josie said.

'Larger than life in more ways than one. One of the local characters, everyone's best friend. I've only met her a handful of times. She won the lottery a couple of years back, so now owns the local launderette, as well as one of the bakeries. She puts her golden stamp on everything.' Hilda chuckled. 'What used to be the Porth Melynos Tea House is now Cathy's Cakes and Buns.'

'I'll be sure to stop by while I'm here.'

'Great for diabetes,' Hilda said, then tapped the tabletop with far more finesse than Cathy had. 'Right, let's order. My stomach is starting to grumble.'

An hour later, filled with curry and a couple of pints of beer each, Josie felt ready to turn in. Hilda, though, defying her years, ordered a bottle of wine.

'I just want to have a proper toast to you being here,' Hilda said. 'Every cloud has a silver lining, and your divorce was definitely mine. I could never get up to Bristol to see you as much as I wanted, what with work and everything, and while this certainly isn't the ideal situation, I think it's great that we can spend some time together.'

'I appreciate having a friend,' Josie said, suddenly feeling a little tearful. 'After everything that's happened, I really needed it. Most people we knew took Reid's side by default, as though the sensitive singer-songwriter couldn't possibly be to blame for anything. My friends turned against me, and even Tiffany—'

She clamped her mouth shut, but it was too late, the alcohol had done its work.

'What about Tiffany? She's still on your side, isn't she? Has she decided where she would like to do her residency?'

Josie felt like the world—or at least one of Cathy Ubbers' hands—was pressing down on her shoulders. She slumped in the chair and sighed.

'She told me she's dropping out. She doesn't want to pursue medicine anymore. After all these years of studying—after all the money I spent to support her—all that work, and she'd decided it's not what she wants.'

'Oh dear. Well, perhaps she'll do something similar, you know, paramedic or something like that—'

Josie could barely bring herself to speak. 'She's decided to be Reid's tour manager,' she said. 'She's turned her back on everything she's worked for to help her father.' She gave a sad chuckle and wiped away a tear. 'I suppose that's something, isn't it? She's loyal to her family. Half of it, at least. Whether he's deserving of that loyalty, I don't know. He was hardly ever there when she was a little girl. Never did sports practices, and the one time he came to parents' evening, he tried to slip her form teacher a CD with his mobile number written on the inside. Oh, he brushed that off, told me it was a spare copy he'd made for a radio station. God, what a fool I was. And now … look at me.'

She realised she was crying. She looked up at Hilda, her vision a blur.

'Oh, Josie—'

'I built a house and it fell down,' Josie sobbed. 'Every last brick. I worked, and I built, and I saved, and I … I … held it all, held it all together, even as all the pieces started to float apart. I held on. Then it blew up in my face, and I ended up with nothing. Is that how life's supposed to be, Hilda? Is it?'

Hilda reached out and patted her on the back of the hand. 'If you're on the ground,' she said, 'You have to try to get to a knee. Because if you can get to one knee, you can get to the other knee, and if you can get up to your knees, you can stand. You need to stand, Josie.'

'I'm standing,' Josie said. 'But sometimes I don't want to stand. I really just want to lie down and close my eyes.'

'And when you open them again, things will have got that little bit better,' Hilda said. 'Because that's the way things work.'

Josie smiled. 'Thank you,' she said.

They fell silent for a few minutes, listening to the gentle background music. The pub had emptied out now that the restaurant had closed. A few people still sat along the bar, leaning into their drinks. Josie listened to the song playing in the background—some old hit, the name of which she couldn't remember—and thought that if Reid's song came on, she would probably scream.

'Nine o'clock,' Hilda said quietly.

'What? It's later than that, isn't it?'

'I'm talking about tomorrow. Nine o'clock start? I can do eight if you really want.'

'What do you mean?'

'I'm going to help you with the campsite. See if we can't get it fixed up.'

'It's too much for you, all that work.'

Hilda smiled. 'I'm not dead yet.'

10

STOPS AND STARTS

IN THE MORNING, having shared a second bottle of wine, it was Josie who was the worse for wear, while Hilda bounced around as though she'd spent the evening drinking carrot juice. As Josie stumbled into and out of the shower, Hilda made them both a large fried breakfast, and then together they headed over to the campsite.

'You'll need to start thinking about logistics soon,' Hilda said, as they walked down the lane, a light breeze blowing over the top of the hedge, a warm sun beaming out of the sky. 'Listing the campsite in newspapers, on the internet, that kind of thing. You'll need shop stock, staff. You can probably get away with a few student workers for most of it. You might need some red tape seen to, but I have a mate on the council.'

Josie glanced at her friend. 'I haven't even cut the grass back yet.'

'When you're driving your car, do you look at the road right in front of you, or do you look further ahead, to see what's coming?'

'I don't have a car.'

Hilda chuckled. 'Oh yes, I forgot. Don't worry, once the money starts rolling in, you can buy all the cars you want.'

'I'd be happy to have my old Volvo back.'

'You have to look to the future, my wonder. What about a new Volvo?'

'I suppose I could go for a new used Volvo.'

'See? Now you're talking. Ah, here we are.'

The campsite looked the same as yesterday. Josie peered into the gloom under the trees, wondering whether her tree-living friends had been up to no good during the night. Everything looked as it should be, however: wild, untended, ruined, an impossibility staring Josie in the face. She set down the bag she was carrying with a sigh, wondering if it was too soon to suggest they break for the flasks of coffee they had brought with them, but Hilda clapped her hands together.

'Right, let's get to work,' she said. 'I'll start pruning those bushes by the entrance. It looks like you have some privet in there, and a bit of blue gem and veronica.' She chuckled. 'Nat must have been quite the garden centre stalwart back in his day.'

'I assume you're talking about plants?'

'Yes. There are some lovely shrubs in here. They're just a bit overgrown, that's all. Nothing a little hard pruning won't fix.'

Josie left Hilda by the entrance and walked down to the barn. At the sight of the door standing just open enough to allow someone entry, however, her hackles began to rise. She clenched her fists, glaring at the door as though to splinter it with her gaze.

'If you've been in there … I'll—'

She peered into the gloom, then stepped inside. She had taken no more than a couple of paces, though, before she stopped dead in her tracks. One of the old table tennis tables, dusted down, had been carried out into the central corridor. Where a net had rotted away, now pieces of plywood made a crude partition.

Something was standing on the table near the net, a small plastic basket. Josie approached cautiously, fearing it might be full of more frogs, but to her surprise it was just four tatty table tennis paddles and a handful of balls. All of them looked stained and water damaged as though they'd been found buried in the undergrowth.

'Oh!' came a voice from behind her, and Josie gasped as she spun round. It was only Hilda, though, standing just inside the barn door with a pair of pruning clippers in her hand. 'Did you set it up already? Why don't we have a quick game?'

'Not me,' Josie said, but before she could launch into some diatribe that it had to be the squatters taking advantage of things, Hilda had hopped over to the basket and selected a paddle.

'Come on, humour an old woman,' she said, swishing the paddle through the air. 'I think I can just about get it over the net.'

'If you insist,' Josie said with a smile. 'I used to play a little with Tiffany when she was younger. I'll go easy on you.'

'You're such a dear.'

Josie tapped down a couple of weak serves and Hilda did her best to hack them back over the makeshift net. After a few minutes of gentle tapping back and forth, Hilda said, 'Right then, shall we have a game?' She grinned. 'How about the loser buys lunch?'

'Sure,' Josie said. 'I liked the look of that steakhouse down by the harbour.'

'Oh, that place is great,' Hilda said with a grin. 'You'd

have to sell another car to afford it, though. All the tourists these days are getting milked harder than Davey Blinchard's flock come Wimbledon strawberries and fresh cream season.'

'Luckily I won't have to,' Josie said. 'Go on, I'll let you serve.'

'You're so kind.'

Josie tapped the ball across the net and Hilda make an awkward show of grabbing it. As soon as she had it in hand, though, she turned her body, lowering her stance, and switched her grip on the paddle. When the ball came flashing back across the net, it dipped sharply and then swung away at such a tight angle that Josie nearly fell over in a vain attempt to even get near to it.

'One zero,' Hilda said, giving Josie a wink.

'You've not gone and sharked me, have you?' Josie said.

Hilda grinned and sent another serve whizzing past Josie's desperate swipe. 'The best bit of sharking since Uncle Phil broke out Lucille,' Hilda said with a delighted chuckle. 'British Under 16s girls champion, 1968. Might have played a bit more had there been any money in it. Come on, though, it's been more than fifty years. I'll tell you what, to make it a little fairer, no spin serves.'

'If I sold my shoes, would I be able to buy us half a steak?'

'I'd settle for a homemade sandwich.'

Josie grinned. 'You're on.'

It wasn't a total walkover. Josie managed to win a couple of points, but Hilda was clearly taking it easy on her, and in the 'more than fifty years since her junior British title' she had lost a bit of mobility.

By the time Hilda had completed a three-games-to-zero whitewash, Josie had come up with another idea.

'We could have a campsite tournament,' she said. 'Or

maybe you could come in and offer a bit of coaching to the kids?'

Hilda gave her a mild smile. 'We'll have to see,' she said. 'But you're starting to think the right way. Listen, I'm sorry to drop this on you, but I need to get back. Something's come up.'

No phones had rung, neither had Hilda glanced at any schedules or planners. Still, she looked suddenly nervous, as though she had left the taps running or the oven on.

'I'll pop down again in the morning to see how you're getting on,' Hilda said.

'What about dinner?'

Hilda gave Josie a hopeful look. 'You'll need a couple of days to plan your sandwich fillings, won't you?'

Josie waved Hilda off as her friend climbed into her van and headed back up towards the road. Feeling suddenly lonely and craving company, she retrieved the radio Nat had given to her and got to work clearing out the undergrowth from around the cabins, cutting away the brambles and nettles with a scythe, the radio sitting on the ground behind her as she worked.

The work definitely wasn't as enjoyable without Hilda around, but Josie took pride in each pathway she cleared of brambles, each cabin that emerged from the undergrowth. Using the keys from the reception to get inside, she found they were in better repair than they ought to be, a little dusty, a little overrun with spiderwebs, and a couple showing evidence of mice having taken up residence, but they were structurally sound, the water worked, and in many the electric also did.

She took a break for coffee. Then, feeling a little braver, she took the strimmer and headed for the clearing under the treehouses.

'Don't mind me,' she said, setting her radio down on

the ground below the treehouses. 'I know you're up there. I saw you'd had a game of table tennis earlier. Why don't you come down and we'll have a chat about things?'

No one answered her. She adjusted the radio on to a music channel since she wouldn't be able to hear it anyway, then got to work with the strimmer, cutting back the long grass and brambles around the edge of the clearing, widening the space, opening up the dramatic, sweeping view of the cove and the headlands below. So spectacular in fact, that she forgot all about the people living in the trees until she swung around to find herself faced with a person literally hanging upside down, arms reaching for her radio.

She switched off the strimmer and set it down by the picnic table. 'Get off that!' she snapped, as the person, feet in some kind of rope brace, grabbed her radio and made a sharp cry to the others in the trees. As the rope tightened, pulling him back up, Josie ran over. Too late, the person had returned to the treehouse, stolen radio in hand.

'That's mine. You give that back!' she shouted, thumping a hand against the tree trunk. Incensed, and ignoring any possible danger, she circled the tree, looking for a way up.

She had just found some old divots cut into the tree which offered possible hand and foot holds, when more movement caught her eye. She turned, just in time to see another figure jump down from a tree closer to the clearing's edge, run to her strimmer, and kick it over the edge.

'You—'

The figure made it back to the tree, grabbed a dangling rope and was hauled swiftly up before Josie could get a hold of him. As she looked up to see a foot disappear over the wooden railing of one of the walkways, she let out a howl of frustration.

'I don't know who you people are, but I'm not having this,' she snapped.

She went to the clearing's edge to look for her strimmer. The slope was steep but it couldn't surely have fallen far. There was no sign of it on the grassy slope, however. She looked further down, and caught sight of it, far below, the heavy machine sliding and rolling as the slope steepened. It was heading for a section of the coast path which had been re-cut around a crumbling section of cliff. Surely the path would stop it, she thought, but as it reached the flatter section, it caught on something in the grass, made a dramatic, comical somersault, bounced right across the path and vanished over the cliff edge.

Josie looked up at the treehouses. 'That's it,' she snapped. 'You want a war … you've got one.'

11
A DIP IN THE SEA

Josie felt certain Hilda would lend her a chainsaw, but not if she had lost her expensive petrol strimmer. Giving the treehouses one last withering glare, she headed down the switchbacks of the path towards the shore below.

It was lucky no one had been on the intersecting coast path when the tumbling strimmer came bouncing past. Perhaps Josie now had grounds to call the local police, get the squatters thrown out of the campsite once and for all.

By the time she had negotiated the private section of path, her thighs ached from the steep descent. She climbed over the rope on to the public coast path, paused to catch her breath, then tentatively peered over the crumbing section of cliff to see how far the strimmer had fallen.

To her dismay, the strimmer had fallen all the way down into the water some fifty yards below. Josie let out a long sigh, wondering what she would tell Hilda. Her friend would likely forgive her for the strimmer's watery demise, but it was a matter of principle. She glanced back up the slope and saw a line of faces peering over the edge of the clearing, watching her.

Josie gave a small shake of the head.

You won't win.

In the divorce court she had fought Reid with everything she had, refusing to let him push through his bogus claims that she had restricted his earning power, that she had held him back in his career. Utter lies, the lot of it, yet somehow the judge, spotted at one point during a break humming one of Reid's songs, had fallen for every last lie and sob story. Reid had got his way in every single decision, and what little Josie had retained went to pay for her lawyer. When their old family house did eventually sell, she would be left with too little to buy a place of her own, perhaps just enough to fritter away on rent for a few years before she was destitute enough to apply for social benefits.

He had comprehensively ruined her, but if defeat in the greatest battle of her life had done anything, it had made her reluctant to lose again.

You will not win.

There was another path that descended to the cove below. Josie made her way down, finding herself on a pleasant but secluded beach. Tiny waves tickled the shoreline, the sea all but becalmed. The grey sand stretched around the inlet until ending at some craggier slate outcrops that backed up against the cliffs, their angles creating a series of narrow inlets.

The strimmer had fallen over there somewhere. Josie marched across the beach, determined to retrieve it, then climb back up to the campsite and give the treehouse people an ultimatum. Either they get out of the trees and leave the campsite, or there would be trouble.

A jagged outcrop of slate stood between her and where the strimmer must have fallen. Josie pulled off her wellington boots and socks, then climbed up onto the rock, wincing as the barnacles and limpets poked into the soft soles of her feet. It must take practice, she realised, to negotiate the rocks on a beach, the way she had seen kids down at Porth Melynos harbour doing it. Her feet were like delicate fairy wings being smashed by a mace, each step bringing fresh agony as she clambered up the steep side of rock.

Reaching the top, she peered over, dismayed to see how it just dropped away into the sea fifteen feet below. The water rose and fell, the swell that didn't seem to bother the beach quite apparent here, lifting and falling like the lungs of some impossibly large machine. With each dip, seaweed-covered rocks were exposed, while each rise brought sprays of white water increasingly close to Josie's face.

The strimmer lay half in and half out of the water on the other side of the gully, its petrol tank caught on a jutting platform of rock. With each swell it shifted; one decent pull and it would drop into the water, perhaps never to be seen again.

Unable to get down without literally jumping into the water, Josie began to shimmy along the top of the slate ridge, hoping to find some way down on the other side, where hopefully it would be shallow enough for her to wade across to the strimmer. The slate ridge only got steeper, though, rising up to join the cliff, the sea sloshing in and out of a cave carved out of the rockface. Aware she might have to swim across, Josie found the flattest section of rock that she could, then pulled off her jeans and jumper.

The sun was warm on her bare skin as she stripped down to her underwear, but each gust of wind brought a chill that covered her skin in goose pimples. Crouched on top of the ridge, she peered down into the water. There was a ledge below her on the other side, low enough that from there she could slide into the water. The strimmer was no more than a couple of feet away on the other side, perhaps within arm's length from the water. And with each pull of the swell, a triangle of stones appeared to her left, meaning the water couldn't be that deep.

It just looked so cold. Josie found herself shivering just at the thought of it. The sensible decision would be to find a way across to the other side and grab the strimmer without going anywhere near the water. As another swell rose, though, the strimmer twisted. One more decent tug and it would be in the water, sinking to the bottom. If the current dragged it out, she would never see it again.

Hilda could afford another; that wasn't the point. She had lent it to Josie in confidence, and Josie had let this happen. She had let a group of weirdos get the better of her, and she'd had enough of being pushed around.

Heart thundering, she climbed down onto the ledge.

The water rose and fell, a gentle pulsing. It looked inviting but terrifying at the same time. Josie lowered her feet over the edge. If she timed it right, perhaps she could get the strimmer before she got too wet—

'What the hell are you doing?'

The voice came out of nowhere. Josie flinched, lost her grip on the rock and plunged like a stone over the edge.

The cold shock was like a hard slap all over her body. Her head went under before she could figure out what was going on, then her feet mercifully touched pebbles and she kicked upwards with all her might. As she broke the surface, she twisted around and saw she was already several feet further out than where she had jumped in. The swell rose, lifting her off the bottom, and she felt the drag of the water as it receded, pulling her out.

'Grab my hand!'

She bobbed again, a few feet further out than before.

She couldn't see any hands, but as she twisted around, she saw a tiny fishing boat bobbing in the water. At first, the figure in the boat was nothing more than a silhouette against the sun, then the water pulled her again, and she recognised Robinson, leaning over the side, one hand outstretched.

'Come on, I've got you,' he called.

Josie, the cold starting to make her dizzy, flapped her feet, searching for purchase, but the seabed was gone. Out of her depth, a sudden panic set in and she began to struggle, arms flailing. She tried to shout for help, but the water rose over her face and salty water filled her mouth. She kicked again, desperate, arms flailing, wishing in her panic to remember the simple ability to swim.

Then fingers closed over her forearm and pulled. Her head rose out of the water and she coughed, spraying salty water over the side of the boat as it bobbed in front of her. Robinson, leaning down, grabbed her other arm and dragged her upwards until she could get her fingers over the boat rail. Holding on with one hand while Robinson held the other, she clambered like a blind, geriatric seal over the edge and rolled unceremoniously into the floor of the boat.

'Well, that wasn't the cleverest idea,' Robinson said. 'Are you all right?'

Josie wasn't sure. She lay curled up in the middle of the boat, shivering with cold, feeling both humiliation at her stupidity, relief at being rescued, and embarrassment over being found in only her underwear, which was all now soaked through.

'It's all right,' Robinson said. 'Here.'

Josie risked a glance up to see him holding out a towel. She stuck out a hand and snatched it like a frightened child.

'I'm sorry, it's all I've got. I mean, you're welcome to my shirt if you like—'

He reached up and started to pull the old polo shirt over his shoulders. She caught a brief glimpse of a toned, tight midriff before she blurted out, 'No, it's okay. I'm fine.'

The boat bobbed in the water. Josie slowly sat up, pulling the towel around her shoulders, trying to cover as much of herself as possible. Robinson, sitting at the stern with one hand on an outboard motor, watched her with a puzzled look. Had she not been so cold, Josie might have flushed with embarrassment. As it was, it was all she could do not to let her teeth chatter with cold.

'Did you leave your clothes in there somewhere? I can take us in to the beach and run over to get them.'

'St … stri … strim … strimm….'

'I'm sorry, is that English? I'm afraid I don't understand. You chose a really bad place for a spring swim. The rip tide is brutal on this side of the cove.'

'Strimmer!'

'What? I don't—'

Josie managed to point, her arm shaking with cold. 'My friend's strimmer … it … it fell in the water.'

'Your friend's strimmer?'

'For … cutting … cutting grass.'

'Ah.' Robinson nodded. 'Ah, right. Hang on, we'll run in and get it.'

He pulled a cord and the outboard started up. In a moment the boat was buzzing into the inlet between the ridges of slate. Josie pointed at the strimmer still hanging half in the water, and Robinson brought the boat in close enough to reach over the side and get a hold of it. He lowered it into the centre of the boat as they bobbed up and down, the swell more powerful now, making Josie only feel more foolish at her attempted rescue.

'Come on, let's get back to the beach,' Robinson said. 'I actually have some sandwiches and coffee. They'll sort you out.'

Robinson steered the boat into the shore, then climbed out in the shallows and hauled it up onto the beach. Only when Josie felt the first sand bumping against the bottom of the boat did she think to get out, rolling awkwardly over the side into freezing cold, knee-deep water. She slipped on a rock and splashed down on her bum, soaking herself all over again, then jumped up with a gasp in time to see Robinson give a little laugh.

'Be careful in there,' he said, dragging the boat up onto the shore, the muscles of his powerful arms pressing through his shirt. 'It's a bit uneven. Not much of a swimming spot, this.'

Josie said nothing, just squeezed out the sopping towel and wrapped it around herself again. It was now wet and cold, but at least it kept the wind off.

'I'll go and get your clothes,' Robinson said, jogging off across the beach before Josie could respond, bare feet moving nimbly from rock to rock. He reached the slate ridge and bounded up the steep, treacherous surface it had taken Josie forever to scramble, walked along the top of the ridge with his arms outstretched like a tightrope walker, then bent down, scooped up her clothes, and came running swiftly back.

'I'm afraid your jeans had fallen into a rock pool,' he said, holding them up to reveal a wet circle on the backside. 'It's a bit too chilly to dry them out in the sun, but if you want, I can lend you mine—'

He started to unbuckle a pair of tatty jeans, but Josie put up a hand.

'No!'

Robinson stopped and looked up. 'All right. Would you like a ride back to the village?'

Josie tried to speak, but no words would come. She wanted to thank him at the very least, but her neck and cheeks were prickling with shame. The best thing to do would be to make an excuse, grab the strimmer and her wet clothes and climb back up to the campsite, then gather a chainsaw or even a can of petrol and a match, and sort out the people in the treehouse once and for all, but all she could do was stare at the grey sand at her feet and wonder if it was easier to sit down than stand up.

She fell more than sat, bumping down onto the sand, the wet towel covering her legs and stomach, hiding as best she could a body that could no longer impress anyone, a body that had been divorced, tossed away, forgotten.

Abandoned, rejected, discarded—

She rolled onto her side, bringing her legs up. A strange, low wailing was coming from somewhere.

She lay there for a long time, the sand actually warm beneath her body, and something else—her jumper—lain over her other side. She wished the ground would absorb her, end her suffering, stop the slow, gradual torment.

It felt like she had been lying there for hours, when she finally found the strength to sit back up and look around. The sun appeared to be in a different place, further across the sky, as though she had fallen asleep in one world and woken up in another.

Robinson was sitting beside her, shirtless, the wind ruffling his hair as he stared out to sea, hazel-brown eyes watching something on the horizon. He looked over as she sat up, took a bite out of a ham sandwich, then held up a plastic cup.

'Coffee?' he said.

12

ANSWERS AND MORE QUESTIONS

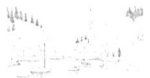

'GRANDAD WAS A WRITER,' Robinson said, tipping the flask to refill Josie's cup. Wearing her own jumper, with Robinson's shirt covering her legs, she was slowly defrosting. Her jeans, hung up between two pieces of driftwood nearby, billowed in the breeze. Robinson, wearing only his jeans, seemed to feel no cold at all. 'Earnest Blackthorne. You won't have heard of him. He never published anything, just put these humongous manuscripts away in boxes in the loft. Growing up I remember him boasting about being the Cornish Charles Dickens, and that one day he'd be discovered, and he'd end up rich. He never was, though. Sadly, he died unknown to the wider world. Dad was inspired enough to name me after Robinson Crusoe, however.'

'Which was written by Daniel Defoe.'

Robinson grinned. 'The look on Grandad's face must have been something. Dad was never much of a reader, except for tide tables. He got it right for my sister, though. Her name's Scarlet, after *The Scarlet Letter*.'

'Did that make your grandfather happy?'

Robinson shrugged. 'Who knows? He was in the ground by the time I was ten. I barely remember him. Dad has all his stuff in a shed somewhere. I remember his legacy rather than the man himself.'

'Perhaps that's for the best.'

'Any interesting characters in your family?'

Josie sighed. 'Dad and Mum were both gone by my late teens,' she said. 'Cancer for one, an aneurysm for the other. Dad went first, slowly, and I think that might have triggered Mum. I waved her off to work one morning, and never saw her alive again. She dropped down dead at her desk.'

'I'm sorry to hear that.'

Josie shrugged. 'It was a long time ago. I'm older than I look.' At her attempted joke, Robinson gave a half-smile, not quite wide enough to convince Josie he saw the funny side. Feeling a little chastised, she said, 'What about your mum? Is she up there in that shack somewhere?'

'Oh, no,' Robinson said, shaking his head. 'She lives in London. My parents were never married, or anything like that. Dad was kind of a wanderer. He wandered into her life long enough to give her a couple of kids, and for a while we were a family of sorts, then he wandered back out again. He kept in touch, mostly through postcards or random phone calls in the middle of the night, but it wasn't until he went blind and needed looking after that I really got back in touch with him.'

'Growing up without a father, that must have been hard.'

'If you knew my dad better, you'd probably decide it was easier without him than with him.' He gave a chuckle and shook his head. 'So … Hilda said you were divorced?'

Josie nearly coughed out the coffee she was sipping.

'Ah, yes. Recently. I mean, we had been separated for several years, but he decided to make it final.'

'That's too bad.'

'Yeah. He spent our time apart improving his lot in life, and when he was fully armed, he came swooping back in to take what he had left behind.' She sighed, wishing she didn't sound so bitter. 'And then half of what I had, too.'

Robinson said nothing. After a long period of silence, Josie glanced up at him. He was still looking out to sea, the wind still ruffling his hair, the sun leaving shadows across the lines of his face. She wondered what he did for a living: something outdoors for sure, judging by how toned his body was, even in, she guessed, his forties. Lifeguarding, perhaps. Maybe he was a fisherman, or even a farmer. Perhaps a landscape gardener. Something honest, salt of the earth.

'The campsite,' she said slowly. 'It's too much for me. It was good of your dad to give me the opportunity, and I know Hilda thinks it's like some kind of challenge I need to overcome in order to you know … find myself again, but it's … too much. If it was just cutting grass, whatever, maybe….'

She began to explain about the people living in the treehouses. For a few minutes, Robinson listened without interrupting, nodding sagely from time to time but saying nothing until Josie gave a flap of her hands and said, 'I really don't know what to do.'

'Let's go and see Dad,' Robinson said. 'We'll find out what those people are doing and have them moved on.' He stood up. 'I suppose we'd better get back.'

He reached out a hand. Josie stared at it for a moment before letting him pull her up. She held on just a little longer as she found her feet, not wanting to let go.

Summer in Sunset Harbour

NAT STIRRED a cup of cabbage water, then sprinkled a little more pepper on the top before taking a long sip.

'Ah.' He grinned through his beard. 'Tis better. Having trouble with the lads down there, are 'e? They're harmless. Just pretend they's not there.'

'But they're causing me trouble. They left a frog in my bag, they pushed the strimmer off the cliff, and they … set up the table tennis tables without … without asking. Oh, and they stole your radio.'

Nat grinned. 'Ha, that'll be Geoffrey, done that. Lad likes the cricket. Just give him a holler, tell him you'll take a chainsaw to his tree if he don't give it back.'

'They have names, do they? And do they have addresses, places to live that aren't in those trees? I'm a little nervous about it, and I can't get anything done if they're going to sabotage everything I do.'

'Safe as houses,' Nat said.

Robinson came into the small, cluttered living room from the even smaller kitchen next door. He handed Josie a cup of coffee and sat down on a wicker stool, setting his cup down on a round glass coffee table, pushing a couple of fishing magazines aside to make space. Josie, sitting on a plastic garden chair opposite Nathaniel, who occupied the only proper armchair in the room, glanced at Robinson for moral support.

'Who are they, Dad? You know, don't you? Are they old friends?'

Nat gave a wistful sigh. 'Ah, those lads, they's all that's left of me tribe.'

'Your tribe? So they are mates of yours.'

'Disciples,' Nat said. 'Started a bit of a cult back in the late eighties,' he said, as casually as though it was something people did every day. 'Just felt like it, you know.' He chuckled. 'The old man, he had that old campsite down there, and I thought it was as good a place as any. Out of the way, like, not bothering no one, no campers about out of season. Made up some rules, picked one of them rocks out there in the sea as the sacred place, all that kind of stuff.' He sipped his drink, a bit of pepper catching on his beard.

'I remember Mum claiming you'd joined a cult,' Robinson said.

'No, boy. Didn't join nothing. I was like the top dog. Made up the rules.'

'And those people down there, they're from your cult?'

'Tis a funny old thing,' Nat said. 'They just started to show up. Soon we had fifty of them down there, living in the cabins, dancing around, making a mess, all that. They just started showing up. But you know, got bored, you see. Decided to wander off.'

'You just wandered off?'

'Yeah, and then it all kind of ended. Came back a year later, they'd all gone.'

'But what about those guys down there in the treehouses?' Josie asked. 'Have they been living down there for the last thirty-five years?'

Nat threw back his head and cackled with laughter. 'Good heavens, no, maid. They've only been down there since March. Someone from back in the old days was posting something on tinternet, then those boys showed up, asked if they could hang out down there, worship old Mike, ha. Get away from the rat race and all that. And I was like, why not? Got nothing else going on down there, have us?'

'Who's Mike?'

'Ah, the god, see. Gotta have a god if you're gonna

have a cult. Saint Michael, him of the Mount down Mount's Bay. Just round about sunset, you can see a bit of a face in the cliff there, across the cove. Looks like a lad peering out of the rocks. Tis St. Michael, so I said. 'Mikey boy.'

'That's madness.'

Nat shrugged. 'Weren't me showing up, wanting to hang out.'

'So, you said they could stay down there?'

'Yeah, why not? Not doing no harm, are they? One of them's a lad from the village. Perhaps you could have a word with 'e about keeping out of trouble.'

'Do they all have names?'

'Geoff, Lindsay, Dennis, and the lad from the village is Barney.'

'All right,' Josie said. 'That's a start.'

'Not doing no harm,' Nat said, sipping on his drink. 'But if they don't start behaving themselves, I'll go and have a word.'

'Thanks.'

13

OVER THE WALL

Josie set the basket down on the ground at the base of the tree. 'Right, you lot,' she said. 'Grub's up. I have pasties, scones, and some Cornish shortbread. If you want it, though, you have to come down and get it.'

No sound came from the treehouses overhead, except for a little gentle creaking that could have been caused by the wind. Josie, hands on her hips, turned to look out at the cliffs as she waited, trying to see exactly what part of the distant headland looked like St. Michael. While the bay itself kind of looked like an old man with a moustache, even when she squinted or blurred her eyes, all the headland looked like was a jagged pile of rocks. Perhaps a little outcrop on the left could be perceived as a nose, perhaps a rounded upper section could be the forehead—

A rustle of sound made her spin round. The basket was eight feet off the ground, its handles caught by a hook made out of a wire coat hanger. Leaning over the wooden guard rail of the platform overhead, a man with a thick grey beard was pulling on a rope attached to the hanger, the basket slowly rising through the air.

'Hey!'

Josie jumped, fingertips just catching the basket's bottom, but not enough to get a decent grip. She stumbled forwards onto her hands and knees as the basket rose over the guard rail. For a moment, the man's eyes met with Josie's, then he ducked out of sight.

Josie sat up and rolled over. Only as she did so, did she feel a stab of pain in her knee where she had landed on a protruding stone. It had cut right through a section of her jeans that was already frayed, digging deep into the skin of her kneecap. Blood pooled in a deep gash, running through her fingers.

As she felt in her pocket for a handkerchief, Josie looked up at the treehouses above her, then thumped her hands on the ground. She opened her mouth to shout something meaningful, but all that would come out was an angry, frustrated scream. When she looked up, four faces quickly ducked back out of sight.

'If Nat doesn't mind them being there, there's not a lot you can do,' Hilda said. 'I mean, you said you offered them the basket of food, so it's not like they stole it by taking it, is it? And you said you tripped over?'

Josie ran a hand through her hair. 'I can't do it anymore,' she said. 'I just can't.'

'I know the local police constable,' Hilda said, a note of desperation in her voice. 'He lives down in the village. Do you want me to have a word?'

Josie, slumped over in the chair, pushed herself upright. 'No, it's okay. I'll go if you tell me where I can find him. I need a walk to clear my head.'

'Oh, he lives down in one of the harbourside cottages,'

Hilda said. 'Do you want me to call him first, just to make sure he's in?'

Josie shook her head. 'I'll surprise him,' she said, forcing a smile. 'That way he'll have less chance to plan his escape.'

THE POLICEMAN, predictably, wasn't home. As Josie gave his doorbell another desperate ring, however, she couldn't help but feel a sense of satisfaction in this latest failure. Like a bout of self-flagellation, she probably deserved it. After all, everything she had tried to do in recent memory had failed. She had tried to be a good mother, a good wife. A good teacher. Even her ability to be a good friend to Hilda was slipping, like a section of cliff about to give way. And being some kind of free spirit entrepreneur resurrecting an abandoned campsite was as laughable as it was sad.

She staggered away from the policeman's cottage, feeling a half-hearted sense of jealousy at how pretty his house was, and wandered down to the harbourside. Too tired even to sit on one of the benches lined up with a view of the harbour and the cliffs, instead she just slumped to the ground, feet dangling over the harbourside wall.

Had the water been more than a gentle trickle or perhaps the fall—five feet at best—great enough to cause any damage, she could have just pitched herself over. As it was, she simply stared down into the murky green, weed drifting in the slow-moving water as though it might present her with an answer.

She could see her own reflection in there, a vague outline of a human, against a backdrop of mockingly cloudless sky, and—

—a looming figure, leaning over her, one hand lifting to push her over the edge—

'Jose! Jose, is that you?'

A heavy hand cracked down on Josie shoulder, and she looked up to see Cathy Ubbers-Benson leaning over her. One hand still lay on her shoulder, the other clutched an enormous bundle of white sheets.

'Oh, hi. Cathy, isn't it?'

The hand clapped down again. Josie suppressed a wince of pain.

'The very same! Oh, you remember! It's like we were born to be best friends. What's this, ice-cream time?'

'Ah, no. I was just thinking about something.'

'Come on, love, tell Auntie Cathy all about it!'

'Auntie' Cathy was at least fifteen years younger than Josie, perhaps more, but the huge, jovial woman couldn't surely make matters worse.

'You don't know where I can find the local policeman?' she asked. 'I'm after some help from emergency services. I didn't want to worry anyone with a call out, though.'

'Love, I don't, but if it's emergency services you need, perhaps my daddy can help. He's a volunteer fireman, don't you know?'

'Really?'

'Yeah, best in the village.' Cathy chortled. 'Only one in the village, but we'll keep quiet about that, won't we?'

Images of siege towers moving up against castle battlements came to mind. Josie looked up. 'I don't suppose I could borrow a ladder?'

CATHY'S FATHER, Colin Ubbers, had one in his shed which Cathy was happy to loan out.

'He won't even notice, the old love,' she said. 'Just give us a holler in the launderette or the pub when you're done with it.'

Leaving Josie standing on the pavement with a fifteen-foot ladder, Cathy hurried off back to work. Thankfully it was a lightweight model, but its sheer size made it awkward as Josie carried it down the village's main street to the harbour and started up the hill. About halfway up, a kind farmer in a tractor offered her a lift, and dropped her off at the top of the campsite road. With a renewed spring in her step, Josie carried the ladder down to the campsite.

No sound came from inside the treehouses as she set the ladder down, then made a couple of circuits of the treehouse community, looking for a way up. Five treehouses, all interconnected with little walkways and rope bridges, some of which looked original, others that had clearly been recently repaired. She could imagine that it had once been a heavenly place for kids to play, with several of the houses comprising two or more floors, rising up through the trees to tower rooms and crow's nests. However, time waited for no one, and as the trees had grown, several of the treehouses had taken on a leaning, distorted look, boards and roofs shifted, nails bent, floors distorted, as the trees continued their gradual expansion.

Extended, the ladder would easily reach any of the walkways, but Josie had never been much good when it came to ladders. Once, while repainting their house back in their better days, she had stuck to the ground floor while Reid had done everything that required standing on a ladder.

She picked a spot with a decent base, flat and firm, then rested the ladder against the walkway railing overhead. Little more than a couple of yards overhead, it was only just out of jumping range.

It only took a couple of steps to make her feel queasy, however. She clung to the ladder for dear life, squeezing her eyes shut as she took one step and then another. Only when she felt the wooden walkway railing brush her fingers did she open her eyes to find herself level with the treehouse.

They had taken pains to waterproof the little treehouses, pinning plastic sheets up to the insides, attaching pieces of plywood threaded with string to make crude doors. Through one that stood open, hooked against the wind on a latch made by a twist of dried vine, she peered into a gloomy space of camp beds, sleeping bags, inflatable mattresses and dirty blankets. A little camping stove stood in one corner, a bucket filled with plastic plates and bowls in another. A pack of cards lay on a foldout coffee table, its packet so ripped and worn it was barely holding the cards inside. Beneath the table, a couple of dozen generic airport thrillers made a wonky stack.

One thing was for certain, however, was that there were no people here. Perhaps they had gone up to see Nathaniel, to beg the old man to lead them again. Or perhaps they had just gone down to the beach for a swim —and rather grossly, to take care of toilet business, since there didn't appear to be anything here they could use. Whatever the reason, that they had left everything behind meant they were certainly coming back.

Not wanting to get caught unawares, Josie started back down. Just as she glanced down at her feet, however, she spotted the radio Nat had given her standing in a corner of the nearest treehouse.

It would only take a moment to get it. Josie took another step up and tried to hook a leg over the railing. It looked easy, and perhaps twenty years ago she wouldn't have had a problem, but now she was older and what she thought she could do and what she actually could do were two distinctly different things. Halfway over, she felt something tweak in her hamstring, causing her to jerk sideways. One foot caught the side of the ladder even as the other fell over the railing, rolling her inside. As she bumped down hard on the walkway floor, the breath knocked out of her, she wheezed as the ladder fell away, landing in the undergrowth with a metallic thud.

Josie lay there for a few moments, recovering her breath. When she could finally draw enough air back into her lungs, she scrambled to her feet and peered over the railing.

The ladder lay in the undergrowth beneath the treehouses. Even though she knew it was only a few feet, and her mind told her it was a few feet, the drop looked like about fifty. Maybe if she could get back over the railing and lower herself down, she could make it, but at the slightest movement her leg sent an electric current of pain through her. Even a short fall could make it worse, and while Hilda might not agree, at Josie's age she might never recover.

She climbed to her feet and hobbled along the walkway to an adjacent treehouse built against the side of a thick oak tree. Here was no different, the remains of a miserable existence inside the cramped hut, but no obvious way down.

Just as she was beginning to come around to the decision that she would have to chance the jump down and hope for the best, she heard voices on the footpath leading up from the beach. She hobbled through another door leading out of the other side of the hut, only to find herself on a walkway that led back around to the first treehouse. She found herself standing next to her radio, so needing an excuse, she reached down and scooped it up, just as a bamboo pole with a hook on the end rose into view, then kept rising until it hooked over something hung in the tree branches overhead.

A rope ladder she hadn't even noticed, attached to the walkway railing along a section that had been reinforced with extra wooden planks to give it more strength. The ladder fell over the side, then the wood began to creak and groan as the squatters hauled themselves up. Josie, clutching her radio, backed up against the railing behind her, watching through the gloomy interior of the treehouse as the first person climbed over, then reached out to help the second person up. Together they helped the third, but instead of waiting for the fourth, they headed straight into the treehouse and sat down around the table, not yet noticing Josie standing outside the other door, the radio held against her chest like a protective shield.

'I'll miss him,' the oldest of the three, a man with a long grey beard that covered most of his face and neck said. 'You never know, he might come back.'

'He was adamant that he was done,' another said, this one a much younger man, his beard undeveloped, mostly just stubble. 'You know, perhaps he has a point. I mean, it was fun while it lasted—'

'Who's for tea?' the third person said, and to Josie's surprise she realised it was a woman of around fifty, but badly aged, looking closer to Hilda's age than Josie's. Her hair was scraggly and knotted, what clothes were visible under the grass sewn into them little more than rags. Her face was narrow, lined, underfed, her eyes bloodshot as though she didn't get enough sleep. This must be Lindsay, Josie surmised, with the old-timer Geoffrey, and the younger man Barney. None of them looked happy; none of them looked pleased to be living in the treehouse.

'Sure, I'll have one,' Geoffrey said.

'If you're making,' Barney added.

Josie cleared her throat. 'If you've got a spare cup … I'd really appreciate one.' As they spun around to look at her, scrambling away from her as though she were a lion about to leap into their midst, she grinned. 'It's been one hell of a day.'

14

CONFESSIONS

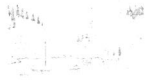

'You can't surely be happy up here,' Josie said, sitting beside the coffee table with one leg tucked up under her and the other—the one she had hurt in the climb up—stretched out to the side. 'I mean ... no offence, but it's totally grotty. And believe me, I know grotty. The last place I had to live in had mould all up the walls. At least it had walls, though. There are holes in yours big enough for birds to fly through.'

'And they frequently do,' Geoffrey said, looking down at his hands. 'We had an owl get in once.'

'Managed to plug that gap with a bit of bark,' Barney said.

'And the spiders and other insects, how do you handle it?'

'Nothing wrong with a few bugs,' Lindsay said.

'If you grow out your beard, it keeps them out of your mouth while you sleep,' Geoffrey said, nodding glumly at Barney.

'That's why I'm growing one,' Barney said, giving Josie an apologetic smile.

'You're a pair of pansies,' Lindsay snapped. 'That extra protein is good for you.'

'Doesn't taste as nice,' Geoffrey muttered.

'Especially when they're still moving,' Barney agreed.

'Can you please stop talking about insects,' Josie said. 'It's bad enough up here during the day. I can't imagine what it's like during the night. Why on earth do you do it? I mean, are you trying to escape the world or something? Considering you're only twenty minutes by bus from a major city, you probably want to try a bit harder.'

'We all have our stories,' Geoffrey said, staring at the floor. 'Me … I was trying to find some meaning to it all. Had the corporate gig, running a little computer chip company. Suddenly it blows up, and I've got money coming out of my ears.' He sighed. 'It was the guilt more than anything. Why do I deserve all this when the next man has nothing? So I blew it. Threw it away on the horses. Sold the company for a fraction of what it's now worth, ended up destitute. Spent my last money on a flight over.'

He had a slight accent which was either South African or German. Josie had never travelled much, so asked him.

'Swiss,' he said. 'You weren't far off.'

'What about you?' she said, turning to Barney. 'Why are you here?'

Barney traced a finger along a grove in the wooden planks. 'Dad's a policeman,' he said. 'He brought us up to follow the law to the letter. Everything we did, everywhere we went, he would go on and on about following the rules and everything would be all right. Then one night last year my sister got killed in a hit-and-run in Plymouth. Dad's a policeman, yet he couldn't stop it, couldn't catch who did it. My sister never put a foot wrong in her whole life. She didn't deserve that, yet it happened anyway. Me, I was flogging pirated stuff on the internet, games, music, films. Making a decent bit of side money. Yet I'm still here. Chloe, she was a perfect, pure soul. Yet she's dead.' He looked up, and the way he stared at Josie made her feel like he expected a genuine answer. 'Why?'

She turned to Lindsay. 'How about you?'

Lindsay, all skin and bones, just stared at the ground. 'What does it matter?'

'We all ended up here for a reason.'

'Did we?' She looked up, glaring at Josie. 'What about you?'

'You want my sob story? It's not much of one, perhaps, but here goes. I was married to a musician. You might know of him; his song was at number two in the charts, the last time I checked. I believed in him, supported him, put my hope in him. I gave him my money, my time, my attention, my energy … and he took it all, and gave nothing back. He found himself a rich older woman and then divorced me, taking everything. I have a few suitcases in a lock up and the clothes on my back.' She patted the radio. 'Oh, and the radio Nat gave me, that you stole.'

'I just wanted to know the score in the Test,' Geoffrey said.

Barney began tapping his fingers on the wooden planks, then started to sing, in a low, gentle voice: 'When I gave up on my wife, I regained my life, now I've pulled those sutures, I can see the future….'

'That's the one,' Josie said with a groan. 'Would you mind not singing it, please?'

'You have to admit it's pretty catchy,' Barney said.

'It's on all the stations,' Geoffrey said. 'I even heard it during a break in the Shipping Forecast.'

'It's still at number two in the charts,' Lindsay said, still not smiling. 'Behind some stupid charity single.'

'He wrote that song while we were still married,' Josie said. 'He said it was a joke, and I forgot about it for years, then suddenly it's gone viral. Now all my friends think I was a terrible wife to him. I lost my teaching job because the school governors sided with the lyrics in a stupid song and said that explained my actions in a certain disciplinary situation. So, if we're playing the My Life is Hell game, I've got a pretty good hand.'

'I think Barney still shaves it,' Geoffrey said. 'His dad's a pig.'

'At least he's alive,' Josie snapped.

'If you can call it that,' Geoffrey said.

Barney sniffed. 'I was thinking … wondering, you know … if I should tell him how I feel.'

'He'll just shoot you down,' Lindsay said. 'That's what all those people do. Shoot others down.'

'He used to read me a bedtime story,' Barney said, sniffing. 'I liked Paddington Bear the best.' He sighed. 'I ripped the newest Paddington film off the Net and flogged it on an auction site to a distributor in China. I made about a grand.'

Josie gave him a small smile. 'You could make yourself feel better if you give that money to charity,' she said.

'I spent it on shoes,' Barney said, not looking up.

'Well, why don't you give those shoes to charity?'

Barney's head lifted. 'Do you think?'

Geoffrey gave him a supportive pat on the shoulder. Josie smiled again. 'Yes. I think that would be a good idea. Or perhaps give them to a children's home or something. I bet none of those kids will ever have worn anything like that.'

'I'm a size twelve.'

Josie grimaced. 'Well, perhaps some of them have big feet.'

'They could use them as flowerpots,' Geoffrey said. 'Avant-garde.'

Lindsay was still glaring at Josie. 'You think you have all of the answers, don't you?'

Josie held her gaze, seeing not only anger there in Lindsay's eyes, but resentment, and a little hopelessness too. Whatever the older woman had been through in life, she felt certain her own troubles paled in comparison.

'No,' she said. 'I don't have the answers. But I think that I'm starting to find some of them.' Then, unable to resist, she added, 'How many answers did Mike give you?'

'Mike,' Geoffrey and Barney said together, both smiling. 'We had a number done on us there.'

'What do you mean?'

Geoffrey chuckled. 'Among other things, St. Michael is the patron saint of banking and the police. We showed up here to escape everything he represents, and every evening he laughs in our face.'

'It's like being in purgatory,' Barney said.

'Is that why Dennis left?'

'Oh, no,' Geoffrey said. 'He just got tired of walking down into the town to scrounge for food every night. Me, I enjoy the exercise.'

Josie stretched out her bad leg, feeling the tug on her hamstring. It felt better than before, a little tight, but she could probably walk on it.

'I saw you'd been in the barn,' she said.

'Only so many games of rummy you can play before you lose your mind,' Barney said.

'Are any of you any good at table tennis?'

'Lindsay has a wicked forehand,' Geoffrey said, to which Lindsay just gave a sharp shake of her head and a hiss of denial.

'Well, my friend is rather good, and I'm terrible. I wouldn't mind a bit of practice. Doubles?'

'Bagsy with Lindsay,' Barney said.

'And afterwards, how about you come to my cabin for something to eat? I have a bit of food in, and perhaps you might be a little more comfortable there than in this treehouse.'

Geoffrey and Barney immediately nodded. Lindsay glared at the floor for a few seconds, before grudgingly saying, 'Well, if you're both going, I suppose I might as well.'

LINDSAY, it turned out, indeed did have a wicked forehand, but her anger made it misfire frequently, and with some steady defensive play, concentrating on getting the ball over the net while waiting for the other pair to make a mistake, Geoffrey and Josie came out narrow winners by two sets to one.

Afterwards, they went up to Josie's cabin, where they set up a little barbeque outside, grilled some burgers and sausages that Josie had bought and even opened a bottle of wine.

'So,' Josie said, a little wine loosening her tongue, asking the question her nose had been dying to ask for the last hour. 'Do you wash in the sea?'

'Sea or the stream down there,' Geoffrey said. 'Every few days.'

Josie wrinkled her nose. 'How about your clothes?'

'Oh, when we get a warm enough day. They don't dry out all that quick when it's cold and there's so much rain in the air.'

'Right. I was wondering about that.'

'Are you trying to say that we smell?' Lindsay snapped, a piece of hamburger falling out of the side of her mouth.

'Um … in a word … yes?'

'We do,' Barney said, head lowered. 'I get a whiff every time I go up that ladder. I mean, you get used to it, and when the wind's blowing through, it's not too bad.'

'Well, the shower block, the one currently engulfed with vines and leaf litter, it still works. There's water. There's even hot water, according to Nat. How about I do you a deal? Help me clear back the weeds and clean it up, and you can use it anytime you like.'

Barney's eyes lit up. 'Deal.'

Geoffrey nodded. 'To be honest, it would be nice to have something to do.'

'Lindsay?'

'I'll think about it.'

'Look,' Josie said, setting down her plate and leaning forward. 'I can go even further. I'm trying to get this campsite up to a standard where it can be reopened. You might have noticed me cutting the grass. You know, before you kicked my strimmer over the cliff.'

'That was Dennis,' Barney said. 'He had a bit of a temper.'

'Well, there's a lot of work to be done. And I really can't do everything. I'd be long gone already if my best friend didn't keep guilt-tripping me into staying.' She stabbed a blackened sausage with her fork and dunked it into a bit of ketchup on the edge of her plate. 'If you were willing to help me get it ready, I'd be willing to give you a couple of the cabins to use. And if we can ever get it tidy enough to open, I'd even be up for splitting whatever money we make.'

Geoffrey watched her over the top of his hamburger. Barney stared into his glass of wine. Lindsay glared at the embers of the barbeque as though trying to make them spit and flare.

'Well?'

'Miss, you don't know how much a proper hot shower and a decent bed would mean right now,' Geoffrey said.

'That's a yes?'

Geoffrey nodded. 'Don't worry about the money, though. It's not important. Just enough to get by.'

'Barney?'

'Hell yes.'

'Great. Lindsay?'

The other woman didn't look up. 'I'll think about it,' she said. However, there was just enough of a hinted smile on her lips to suggest she was thinking about it very strongly indeed.

15

A LITTLE MATCHMAKING

SHE PUT Barney and Geoffrey together in Cabin Two, with Lindsay in Cabin Three. Both cabins needed a little cleaning and tidying, but working together they had them all ready by the afternoon of the day after the agreement. Geoffrey and Barney worked like men trying to claw their way out of a pit, and although Lindsay was a little more stand-offish, she did relent enough to take a cloth and wipe down some surfaces.

The shower and toilet block took a bit more effort. Barney, it turned out, had spent a year as a trainee plumber before dropping out to pursue a less admirable dream of making dubious money on the internet, and the knowledge he had learned was enough to get the pipes clear, the taps running with clean water, and the drains emptying. Of three shower cubicles, only one of the water heaters still worked, but everyone took turns to use it while Josie made a list of things needing to be fixed, the broken heaters at the top.

The jobs that needed to be done got done far quicker with four people working rather than one, and within a couple of weeks they had cut back most of the undergrowth, cleared out the camping pitches, and cleared the vegetation off the remaining cabins. With May bringing warmer weather and longer evenings, Josie began to dream that she might just get the campsite open after all.

'I'm so pleased it's going well,' Hilda said, sipping coffee as they sat at a corner table in the Sunset Harbour Coffee and Fudge Company, a pleasant little café and confectionary shop on the main street that led down to the harbour. 'I was worried you would give up.'

'I can't guarantee that I won't,' Josie said. 'It's still a work in progress. The guys are really helping me out. Well, two of them, at least. The other one….'

'Lindsay, isn't it?'

'Yeah. I mean, some days she's with us; other days she's not. I try to give them a routine, you know, start at nine every day, but some days Lindsay won't come out of her cabin at all.'

Hilda looked down at the crumbs of a piece of fudge cake, and gently tapped the edge of her plate with a fingernail.

'I wouldn't press her too hard,' she said. 'You don't know what she might have been through.'

'That's what I was thinking. I'm happy enough for her to not be disruptive.'

A young waitress came over to their table. 'Are you guys okay over here? Anything else?'

Hilda looked up and smiled. 'No, thank you, Rachel. We're—' Her fingernail tapped the plate again. 'Actually, no. We'll have two slices of treacle tart with cream and two more coffees.'

'No problem.'

As the waitress went off to get their order, Josie gave Hilda a wide-eyed stare and a shake of the head. 'Are you feeling all right? That much sugar will give us both a heart attack. I only just got through that fudge cake.'

Hilda grinned. 'Go on, live a little. Don't worry, we'll burn it off walking back up that hill.'

JOSIE NEEDED to stop in at Nat's place to make a few requests regarding the campsite, so she left Hilda down in the town where her friend said she planned to do a little trinket shopping. With her legs now hardened to long periods of activity, Josie hiked up along the coast path, enjoying the dramatic scenery, passing the fork that led up to the campsite and continuing on to another that led back up to the road through Nat's field.

The old man was outside, tinkering with his carvings, one of which had gained a couple more songbirds since Josie had last visited. All sunglasses and beard, Nat hummed quietly to himself as he hacked away at the driftwood with a chisel, seemingly navigating by feel alone. As she approached, Josie found herself looking around for Robinson, and feeling a twinge of disappointment that he was nowhere to be seen.

'Campsite lass? That you?' Nat called while Josie was still a dozen yards away. Nat grinned. 'I can tell by you's footsteps.'

'It's me,' she said.

'How you doing with the old girl down there?'

'If you're meaning the campsite, then it's getting there. You know I managed to tame your treehouse people enough to get them to work for me. Well, with me.'

'Ah, resourceful, I knew you was,' Nat said. 'Hil said as much. Not sure I'd have agreed if you'd been the townie slacker I'd expected.'

'Um, that's good to know. Anyway, I have this list of things that we need to do, and things that I need your permission to do, since it's technically your campsite—'

Nat waved a hand. 'As you wish, maid. Anything you need, just skim the cost off me cut of the profits.'

'Ah, but I can't do that because I don't actually have any money to get these things in the first place.'

Nat chuckled. 'Ah, maid. See the cabin over there, see the door, no hinge, all that? There's me income. Can't you ask old Hil to lend you a quid or two?'

Josie grimaced. While no doubt Hilda could afford to hire someone to repair the boiler or pay the website setup costs and newspaper advertising fees they would need just to let anyone know there was a campsite here, she hated to ask.

'The most pressing thing is probably the hot water and the rewiring for the shop cabin and the play barn. If you could just—'

'Aha,' Nat said, clicking two crusty sunbaked fingers with a dull thud. 'The lad knows his way around a spanner. I'll send him over when he gets back.'

'Robinson? He's not here?'

'Nope. Gone back up to the smoke. Visit his ma, do a few odd jobs.'

'Right.' Josie nodded. 'Well, thanks for letting me know. If you could send him over—'

'Maid's divorced, ain't 'e?' Nat said abruptly, still peering skyward as though talking to someone hovering above him.

'Um, yes.'

'Nice lad, is me boy. Level headed, can fix anything.' Nat grinned. 'I mean, I can't see what kind of state you're in, but Hil reckons you're a decent catch. You's have a nice voice, soothing, like.'

'Um, I need to go—'

'And a bit of gumption, some meat on you's bones, judging by all that strimming Hil says you've been getting into. Reckon I should have a word with the lad, see if we can't get a bit of a date on the go.'

Nat began to chuckle to himself. Josie, certain there was little more to be gained from her visit, began to retrace her steps.

'Had a bit of a habit of wandering off,' Nat said, just as Josie was preparing to make a break for freedom. The tone in his voice made her pause. 'Couldn't help meself, see?' Nat continued. 'Was born in the bow of me old man's fishing boat, so they say, born with motion in me bones.' He sighed. 'The lad's ma deserved a little better.'

'I suppose things are how they are,' Josie said, trying to be diplomatic.

'When you ain't got much catchment area, you's tends to pick the plot of land that looks prime at the time,' Nat continued, 'thinking them harvest gonna be sweet for donkey's years, then he goes and dries up after a couple.'

'I—'

'"Twas the lad's ma,' Nat said with a gentle, remorseful sigh. 'Country girl like her should have done better than an old plot of land like me. Weren't much use tilling after the first couple of years. I gave her the lad and the lass, but otherwise, didn't give her jack but strife.'

'I need to get back,' Josie said. 'Those weeds won't pull themselves.'

'Lad ain't a bit like me,' Nat said. 'I mean, he goes wandering off up to the smoke from time to time, but he always comes back.'

AFTER SAYING GOODBYE TO NAT, then leaving him to continue lamenting the failures of his life, Josie headed back to the campsite. While Robinson seemed nice, and she had to admit to having been disappointed by his absence, the brutal divorce, her ex-husband's ruthlessness, and even worse, the betrayal of her daughter, were wounds still too open for Josie to consider papering them over with a new relationship. Even if Robinson was interested—and if he saw the same person that she saw in the mirror every morning then she doubted it—they surely wouldn't fit. He was an odd job man, up and down the country, and she was a—what was she even? The manager of a closed, abandoned campsite?

She had no money other than a few scraps left in her bank account. She had three de facto employees to which she had given empty promises, and no real idea of how she was going to pay them anything once the novelty of not having to sleep rough in a treehouse had worn off.

Her boots felt suddenly heavy, as though she were trying to walk through quicksand. When she closed her eyes, all she saw was a black tunnel with no light at the end.

Intending to stop in on Hilda before returning to the campsite, Josie walked up to the main road. She also wanted to check her phone for any messages, since the harbour, the campsite, and Nat's place were all blackspots. Just as she exited the gate onto the road, however, her phone not only began to beep with missed notifications, but to buzz with an incoming call.

Josie pulled it out of her pocket and looked at the display. 'Huh. Well I ... hello?'

'Mum? Mum, is that you?' came a familiar and welcome but all too rarely heard voice. 'I've been trying to call you for ages. That floozy old mare Evangeline, she fired me. Said I wasn't fit for call centre work, let alone tour promotion. Mum, I—'

'Tiffany, dear, it's all right.'

'I don't know what to do, Mum. I just kind of ran out. I'm sleeping in the bus station waiting room. Can I come up to Bristol and stay with you?'

'Ah, I'm not in Bristol anymore.'

'Where are you?'

'Um, kind of down on the coast. Porth Melynos.'

'Did you get a holiday cottage?'

'Something like that.'

'I'm coming, Mum. I'll be there in a couple of hours. I'll give you a call when I get there. Thanks, Mum. I knew I could count on you.'

The call ended before Josie could say goodbye. Tiffany's words rang in her ears. *Count on you. Count on you. Count on you…*

'She's my daughter,' she said aloud, slamming the door on any kind of resentment. *You took his side on everything. You quit the medical school I paid for to support him. You haven't once asked me how I feel about everything.* 'She's my daughter.'

16

THREADS UNRAVELLING

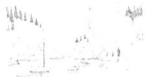

Hilda winced a little as she got out of the chair to fetch the coffee filter. 'I think it's lovely,' she said. 'I can't wait to meet her.'

'I was just getting a hang of things, and now this,' she said. 'I mean, of course she's my daughter, but she took Reid's side in everything. She believed every manipulative lie he told her.'

'And now's your chance to reverse the damage. This should be a positive experience for you, Josie.'

'I know, it's just….' Josie clenched her fists and wrung her hands. 'Argh!' She grinned. 'It's all so stressful.'

'Shall we go down and get another slice of fudge cake after she arrives?'

'Are you sure? You'll be diabetic in a couple of months at this rate.'

Hilda's smile briefly dropped before returning again. 'We can't not celebrate your daughter arriving in Sunset Harbour, can we?'

The call came about half an hour later. Tiffany's bus would arrive at the stop by the harbour about half past three. With a few hours to kill, she headed back down to the campsite.

She met Barney by the entrance, scrubbing and polishing the welcome sign. Much of the paintwork had chipped or flaked off; another job to be added to the list. As Barney paused to greet her, she noticed his beard had gone, and his hair was trimmed. His clothes, benefitting from a solid wash after Josie had called Cathy Ubbers and ordered a collection, looked clean and neat. On his feet he wore a new pair of wellington boots.

Josie couldn't help but smile. He now looked like a regular employee rather than an escaped convict.

'We've started work on clearing the old parking area,' he told her as she came over. 'Under all that brush, there's actually regular grass, believe it or not. Geoffrey suggested we paint some rocks to mark the way in using pastel blue and pale orange, to give the customers a bit of a beachy feeling.'

'Good idea.'

'We'll need paints.'

Josie sighed. 'All right. I'm on it.'

She turned, just as the reception door—newly repaired—opened and a tall, grey-haired man stepped out.

'Excuse me, what are you doing?'

The man started at the sight of her, then his wizened old face opened in a wide smile. 'Ah, Josie. You're back.'

'Geoffrey?'

He reached up to rub his chin as he came over. 'Had a bit of a trim,' he said. 'The lad over there helped me. Huh. Not felt this smooth since I was a kid.'

The shave and haircut, as well as leaving him unrecognisable, had taken years off him. Now, rather than an eighty-year-old homeless man, he now looked like a sixty-something bank manager on the cusp of retirement. Hair ranging from dark grey to white was neatly combed over, hollowed cheeks and an impressively carved jawline held a couple of liver spots and blemishes that claimed his age.

He cocked his head as she watched him. 'What do you think Lindsay will say?' he said, sounding remarkably childlike, reborn even.

'Where is she?'

'Still in her cabin.'

'She didn't come out today?'

Geoffrey's smile dropped as he shook his head. 'I'm afraid not.'

Josie nodded. 'I'll go and see her. It's … nice to meet you again, Geoffrey.'

'And you.'

She left Geoffrey and Barney by the entrance and headed over to Lindsay's cabin, a short distance past the one shared by the others, a little further into the woods.

Josie went up to the door and knocked.

'Lindsay? Are you all right in there?'

A shuffling came from inside as though Lindsay were moving towards the door. The floor creaked, but the door stayed closed.

'Lindsay?'

'I'm fine, leave me alone,' came a muffled voice from inside.

'You don't sound it. Are you sure?'

'Yes. Go away.'

'All right, if that's what you want.'

Josie took a couple of steps backwards, then stopped again, watching the door. No further sound came from inside the cabin.

Josie waited, slowly counting to ten. She had reached

nine when the handle twisted and the door opened. Lindsay, still wild-haired and dressed in little more than rags, peered out. She spotted Josie standing on the path, let out a groan and slammed the door shut.

'Just leave me alone,' she shouted through the door.

Josie said nothing, just stood where she was on the path. After a couple of minutes, she heard Lindsay's voice, but quieter this time: 'You're still there, aren't you?'

'Yes.'

The door opened again. Lindsay, barefoot, stepped outside, closed the door, and sat down on the stone steps in front of the cabin.

'It's my mother's birthday,' she said, eyes on the gravel at her feet.

'Why don't you call her?'

Lindsay shook her head. 'It's been twenty-seven years.'

Josie walked over and sat down beside her. 'That's a long time,' she said.

'Yeah.'

They sat in silence for a while. A thousand things she could say came to mind, but none seemed anything more than hollow advice from someone who had no clue as to the situation. *Just call her.* Was it that easy? Twenty-seven years was a long time to be estranged from someone. Not something to be taken lightly, brushed off, repaired with a simple phone call. And who was she to give advice? She couldn't even manage her own life.

The wind rustled through the branches of the trees overhead. May had been unseasonably warm and the last week had been dry, but under the trees, out of the sun, the wind still carried a chill.

'I….' Lindsay began. 'I … I didn't….'

Josie said nothing. She sat in silence, feeling the breeze

on her cheeks, neck and bare arms, wondering if it could fix her, whether it could fix them both.

'I … I didn't mean … I didn't want … to … be so angry.'

Whether she meant angry at Josie, angry at her family, angry even at herself, Josie didn't know, nor felt she had permission to ask. She nodded to show she had heard, then waited, wondering if Lindsay would open up further.

'It … it was always that way,' Lindsay said at last. Josie glanced up, saw the older woman looking out into the forest. 'I just … things … I felt … frustrated.'

Josie smiled. She understood.

'I wasn't … the best … daughter,' Lindsay continued. 'I wasn't the best … mother. And I … wasn't the best … wife.'

Josie looked down at the backs of her hands. She rubbed at a blemish that had appeared on her skin just behind the knuckle of her ring finger. The skin there no longer felt so supple either, as though it took time to fall back into shape. She glanced at Lindsay and suddenly saw herself in twenty years' time if she didn't take the actions to change things now. She wanted to offer the older woman advice, but perhaps there was nothing she could say that Lindsay didn't already know.

'I was wondering about something,' Josie said quietly. 'That old helter-skelter. I was wondering whether you can see over the top of the trees? Shall we go and find out?'

For a few seconds, Lindsay neither replied nor moved. It had taken an effort for Josie to speak; if Lindsay hadn't heard, she doubted she could muster the strength to repeat herself. She waited, again counting silently to ten.

She had reached eight when Lindsay stood up. 'Let me just put some shoes on,' she said.

17

STICKING TOGETHER

Tiffany looked dressed for mid-winter, with a scarf wrapped around her shoulders and a designer woolly hat pressing bunches of curly, unruly hair against the sides of her face. She peered out of round spectacles as she alighted from the bus, giving a wide grin at the sight of Josie standing under the bus shelter, arms open wide.

'There you are,' Josie said, and all her fears and nerves evaporated as Tiffany let out a squeal of delight and practically danced down the steps and into her mother's arms.

'I'm sorry, Mum,' Tiffany mumbled into the shoulder of the windcheater Josie wore.

'What for?' Josie muttered, holding her daughter tight, not wanting to let go.

'For everything.'

'Sweetheart, you're my little girl. Nothing you do will change how I feel about you. You know that, don't you?' Even as she said it, Josie felt a pang of regret for some of her thoughts. In absentia it seemed far too easy to create an internal agenda. Now, face to face with her daughter, none of the fears and doubts mattered any longer. Tiffany was her daughter, for better or worse, and Josie would love the girl to the ends of the earth, no matter what.

'I should have listened to you.'

Josie pulled away, then patted Tiffany on the cheek. 'Well, you'll have plenty of time to listen to me now, won't you?' She grinned. 'How is your father and his … new lady, anyway? Are they planning to get married now that he's officially … unattached?'

Tiffany rolled her eyes. 'Well, Dad was hoping to.'

Don't bash him in front of Tiffany, no matter what he might have said about me. Two wrongs, and all that. 'I'm sure they're in love.'

Tiffany laughed. 'Oh, don't be silly. I mean, she must be sixty at least, and with all that tanning she does, she looks like a prune. I don't get it. Is she trying to burn all the wrinkles away? The old crone is going to need a full skin transplant at the rate she's going.'

'So, what happened?'

Tiffany rolled her eyes and scoffed. Putting on a pretty accurate toff accent, she said, 'Oh, darling just sign this prenup and we'll all good to go.' She grinned. 'It was at that point that Dad decided he really didn't want to get married after all.'

'Oh well, I suppose at least you don't need to fork out for a new dress now.'

'I prefer jeans anyway.'

'Well, I think you look lovely, whatever you wear.'

'Thanks, Mum.' Tiffany leant in and gave Josie a kiss on the cheek.

'My goodness, how long have you been taller than me?'

Tiffany gave Josie that disbelieving roll of the eyes again. 'Since I was fourteen. Come on, Mum.' She grinned. 'Although I'm wearing platforms. They add an inch or two.'

Josie looked down at her daughter's feet, at a pair of shiny black shoes that appeared to have a sole three-inches thick.

'I think you might be better off in wellies where we're going,' she said. 'Although first of all, we're going for coffee and cakes.'

'Vegan, gluten and wheat-free, one-hundred percent organic?' Tiffany said, raising an eyebrow.

'Nope. Ninety-percent sugar, five-percent synthetic flavouring. I think the walnuts might have come from an actual tree, though perhaps via a packet.'

Tiffany grinned. 'Good. It can get so tiresome living in the city.'

HILDA WAS WAITING for them in the Sunset Harbour Coffee and Fudge Company, and did the surrogate-grandmother thing to perfection, fussing over Tiffany, how much she had grown since their last meeting some years before, her hair, her clothing, how thin she looked, and how she needed an extra-large slice of fudge cake to 'put some meat on your bones.'

Josie had avoided talking about the elephant in the room, that Tiffany had dropped out of medical school, for fear that it might anger her daughter and sour the rebuilding of their relationship, but Hilda had no such qualms.

'It's not that I've quit for good,' Tiffany said. 'I just needed a little time away. The pressure was getting to me. Going straight from all that studying and exams straight into a residency … I just needed a little downtime.'

It was music to Josie's ears, but at the mention of pressure, she felt a dome of motherly protection lowering over her daughter. After all, the pressure she had felt as a teacher had at times been punishing, like wearing blinkers, pushing away the outside world. During particularly busy periods, and especially around exam season, she had struggled to give Tiffany the attention she had needed, justifying it at the time by the fact that her husband had been a stay-at-home 'creative', even if now she suspected the only things he had created were a few diss-tracks towards his hardworking wife and possibly even a couple of secret half-siblings for his daughter. On the latter, Josie had no proof, however; Reid's fame wasn't yet widespread enough that anyone had come out of the cracks to claim his parentage in the tabloids. She wouldn't put it past him, though.

Hilda waved over the young waitress. The girl lifted a notepad to write down their next order, but Hilda instead patted her on the arm.

'Rachel here's fiancé is a doctor, isn't that right, dear?'

Rachel nodded. 'That's right.'

'Maybe he could talk to Tiffany, pass on a bit of wisdom.' To Rachel, she said, 'My surrogate great-niece here is in medical school but finding it a little hard going.'

Rachel nodded. 'William said it was a total nightmare. If you want a chat, he's coming over to the pub tonight.' She grinned. 'Those are awesome shoes, by the way.'

'I got them online.'

'Can I get the site off you?'

'Sure.'

'Before you two get into too much fashionista talk, can we get two more slices of Cornish heavy cake?' Hilda asked.

'Sure.'

Josie leant across and patted Hilda on the arm. 'Steady on.'

Hilda just grinned. 'For the hill, Josephine,' she said. 'For the hill.'

In the end, however, with Tiffany's luggage to carry, they caught the bus back up to the top of the hill. Hilda got off a couple of stops earlier and waved to them as the bus departed. Josie, watching her old friend as she walked away, couldn't help but feel a pang of worry at the sight of Hilda using a stick, the way she had started to wince as she walked. Soon, though, the bus had turned a corner and the campsite entrance was just up ahead.

'You might be a little surprised at where we're staying,' Josie said. 'It's a little … rustic.'

'As long as you have Wi-Fi, we're all good.'

'Ah, yeah, we need to talk about that. Do you remember that time we went camping when you were a child?'

'Not with happy memories. I fell in a ditch and there was construction work going on in the field next door. They were installing a septic tank, I believe?'

'Yes … something like that. Well, now's your chance to overwrite those memories with some happier ones. At least I hope so. Right, this is our stop.'

They got down from the bus. Josie offered to carry Tiffany's bag, but the girl was insistent. As she hobbled along in her platform shoes, Josie wondered whether she should have already got some wellies down in the village. At least the ground was dry.

As they reached the trees at the bottom of the slope, Barney, Geoffrey and—to Josie's surprise, Lindsay— stepped out from behind the entrance sign and waved.

'Welcome, Tiffany, to the Porth Melynos Caravan and Camping Park.'

They began to clap.

'My staff,' Josie said. 'This is Geoffrey, Lindsay and Barney. Although, technically, for the time being, at least, they're all volunteers.'

Tiffany stared. Josie waited, fearful her daughter might drop her bags and attempt to run away. Tiffany peered under the trees, eyes wide behind her spectacles.

Josie, unable to keep her silence, muttered, 'Please say something….'

'Oh, man,' Tiffany said at last. 'This is awesome. Are you the manager?'

Josie grimaced. 'I suppose, technically. But it's becoming more of a joint project. We're hoping to be able to open by the middle of June, although at the rate we're going, it'll be the middle of June … next year.'

'Wow,' Tiffany said. 'Do you have an adventure walk?'

'A what?'

'Like a forest trail with secret stuff for kids to find?'

'Ah, I don't think so.'

'I'll make it. And do you have a mascot?'

'A mas … sorry, what?'

'Mum, come on. You have to have a mascot for stuff like this. A cute badger with a t-shirt or something like that. Woodsie, that would be a cool name. He could have a mate, like a little sparrow who sits on his shoulder. We can call her … Flutterby. Don't worry, I'll design them. Have you got somewhere I can plug in my computer?'

'Ah, electricity is still a work in progress.'

'Hey,' came a voice, making them all turn. Robinson, carrying a toolbox in one hand and a rucksack in the other, came striding down the path. His shirt was unbuttoned to the navel, his body, as well as his shirt, flecked with paint.

'Did I hear someone mention electricity? Dad gave me a call, said you needed some wiring done. I've done a bit of wiring myself, thought I'd come over and see if I can help.'

As he set down his toolbox on the ground, Tiffany leant close to Josie. 'Mum, who's he?'

'Oh, the son of the park owner,' Josie hissed in reply through gritted teeth.

'He's a total dish. I mean, he's waaaaaaay too old for me, but he would be perfect for you.'

18

MAKING CONNECTIONS

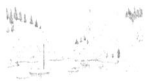

THE SOUND of a strimmer came from through the trees. Behind Josie, someone else was hammering away in the barn. Wading through an area of weeds that was yet to be given the manicure treatment, Josie reached the bottom of the helter-skelter and started up.

The stairs, the broken boards now replaced with new ones, wound up and up. Even though several weeks of manual labour had toughened Josie somewhat, she still found herself puffing as she turned a corner to reach the little viewing platform at the top of the slide.

A rope hung across the top of the slide itself. Gummed up with years of accumulated leaf litter, she hadn't yet checked it for safety, and while Tiffany had volunteered to be a guinea pig, Josie hadn't allowed it. Robinson had a mate who would come and have a look sometime in the next week.

Lindsay stood at the top, a paintbrush in hand, a pot of red paint by her feet, as she carefully touched up the designs that had faded over the long years of disuse and abandonment.

'How's it going?' Josie asked, as the older woman turned and gave her a smile.

It seemed strange to think of overalls flecked with paint as an improvement, but compared to Lindsay's previous rag-like attire, it was significant. Lindsay turned to look at Josie. Her face had lost its hardness, her cheeks no longer quite so hollow, filling in some of the lines with a touch of vitality. She would never be young again, nor even flush with it, but she now looked closer to Josie's age than Hilda's. Her hair, light brown streaked with grey, after a cut and styling now looked fashionable rather than unruly.

'I called them,' she said, then lifted a hand to wipe away a tear. 'Barney lent me his phone. Last night, I called all of them.'

Josie found herself welling up. 'How on earth did you get reception?' she asked, choking back a sob.

Lindsay smiled. 'I sat right here. You can get a solid five bars.'

'That's great.'

'We talked. I'm going back in the summer for a couple of weeks. Do you think you'll be able to manage?'

'We'll be fine. We'll hold your cabin for you, though. I'm hoping to stay open right through September if the weather stays good.' She grinned. 'Target the retirement age group, maybe, once the kids have gone back.'

'Thank you,' Lindsay said.

Josie shook her head. 'I literally did nothing. This was all you.'

'You listened. Most people just talk and talk and talk. I just needed someone to listen. Thank you.'

Josie came forwards and the two women shared a hug. 'No worries,' Josie said.

'Oh, something else,' Lindsay said, pulling away. 'Geoffrey asked me to go and get ice cream with him one evening. What do you think?'

'Geoffrey … ice cream? Wow, that's … smooth.'

'I mean, he looks better without the beard. Tidier. He's about ten years younger than I thought, too.'

'Do you like him?'

Lindsay grinned. 'I spent two months living in a treehouse with him. I think if I didn't, I might have pitched him over the railing at some point.'

'Box one ticked. Do you like ice cream?'

Lindsay rolled her eyes. 'Who doesn't?'

'Then go for it.'

Lindsay lifted an eyebrow. 'I'll wait and see if he asks again. Check if he's keen or not.'

'Nothing like being a teenager again, is there?' Josie said with a smile.

'We're all going to die eventually,' Lindsay said. 'I suppose we'd better make the best of things while we can. Mistakes, and everything else.'

Josie said goodbye to Lindsay and headed back up to the reception and shop, where she found Tiffany sitting behind a nearly installed desk which smelled of pine and resin. A fashionable ladies' cap perched on top of her head as she hunkered down over a laptop computer.

'Aha, got it. And we have … a connection!'

'Everything going okay?'

Tiffany looked up. 'Perfect. Now we have a net connection, I can start working on the website and getting us on all the listings sites. Are you ready for the flood?'

'Of people, I hope.'

'Once I work a bit of SEO magic, we'll be everywhere. I'm about to put Porth Melynos Caravan and Camping Park on the virtual map.'

'That's great. You know, it was a godsend you coming

here. I could never have done all this stuff without you. Scrubbing and sweeping is about all I'm capable of.'

Tiffany frowned. 'Don't sell yourself short, Mum.'

'I'm not—'

'Just because Dad and you weren't compatible, doesn't mean you're not capable of anything you want to do.'

'Shouldn't it be me telling you things like that? And what do you mean, we weren't compatible?'

'Honestly, I don't know how you stayed together so long. You're so different. I know when I was a kid, I saw it all through rose-tinted glasses, but you know, I'm older now. I can see the cracks. You should have broken up years ago. I appreciate that you made the effort for me, though.'

Josie flapped her hands, trying to think of the right thing to say. 'It wasn't that … it was just … I don't know, a case of just keep your head down and carry on, hope things work out.'

'Yeah, that's the old way of doing things, and its commendable, I suppose. Don't tell me you're not happier now, though.'

'Happier, maybe. Definitely not better off. I mean, I have to shower in a shared toilet block a five-minute walk from where I sleep. And come autumn, I might be homeless again.'

'Bridges, Mum. It's all just bridges to cross.'

Josie smiled and patted Tiffany on the shoulder. 'I sent you off to university all bright-eyed and innocent, worried you'd get drunk on your first night and forget where you lived—ha, kind of like I did—and five years later you came back, but thirty years older.'

Tiffany lifted an eyebrow and tugged at a curl of hair. 'Can you see any grey ones yet?'

'You're good.'

'Must be the dye. So long as you can't tell I'm an old

biddy. By the way, I'm going down to the pub tonight if you want to join. Me and Barney are meeting Rachel and her fiancé. You know, the doctor? I mean, there might be a bit of shop talk, but that won't take long. Apparently they've got a comedian coming in, some localish girl from up Willow River way. Come on, it'll be a laugh.'

'I appreciate the thought, but let me take you a step back there. You and Barney?'

'Mum … we're just mates. I mean, look at my options. You—my mother—Lindsay or Geoff. Much as I like them….' She flapped her hands. '…. I don't want to hang out. Barney wins by default, but it just so happens that he's cool.' Tiffany clicked her fingers. 'Bonus.'

'Mates?'

'Mum, I'm on a bit of a life rebound, don't you know? Just fun for the time being. You don't need to worry.'

Josie sighed. 'You're a wonderful daughter.'

'Of course I am. I got half of your genes and the good half of Dad's. So what's your excuse for pub-avoidance anyway?'

'I'm meeting Hilda. She wants to take me somewhere.'

'Sounds exciting. Well, have fun. And if you get back in time, you know where to find us.'

Josie left Tiffany to her computer work and went back to her cabin to change. Hilda had said only to wear something warm and suitable for walking. Hilda put on her wellies and grabbed her coat, then headed up to the main road to wait.

She didn't have to wait long. Hilda came hammering around the corner on her motorbike and pulled up beside Josie. She lifted her aviator's googles and grinned at Josie.

'Need a ride?'

'Where are we going?'

'You'll see.'

Hilda headed inland, and half an hour of wild driving later, the grey-green rise of Dartmoor appeared in front of them.

'Hound Tor,' Hilda said, when they stopped at a petrol station. 'One of the best sunset views in Devon. I've always meant to go but never got around to it.'

'You're expecting me to go walking on Dartmoor in wellies?'

Hilda grinned. 'At least you don't need a stick.'

It seemed like a ridiculous plan, setting off for the peak of Hound Tor at five o'clock in the evening, armed only with some warm coats, a flask of coffee, some sandwiches, a compass, a pair of torches, and some spare batteries, just in case. Yet, as Hilda, walking with a stick, set a pace that Josie struggled to match, she could only marvel at her friend's spirit. Josie, concerned that they would get lost in the dark, had voiced her concerns to Hilda, only for her friend to produce a red beacon light which stuck with tape to the motorbike's petrol tank.

'This is a nifty little thing I got on the internet,' she said. 'It comes on after dark, and it also has an alarm attached. It'll guide us home and keep any would-be thieves off my bike. Right, off we go.'

Hilda, for all her initial enthusiasm, started to tire as they neared the tor. By the time they reached the rocky outcrop, Josie was supporting her by one arm, and helped her to sit down on a flat section of rock with a view to the west where the sun hung low in the sky.

'Phew,' Hilda said, wiping her brow. 'We made it.'

'I think you're mad,' Josie said. 'I didn't think you were going to get up that last steep bit.'

'Ah, all downhill from here,' Hilda said, pointing at the distant car park down in the valley, where their motorcycle and sidecar was a tiny speck alongside a handful of other cars. 'Right, let's get that coffee out.'

Josie did the honours, and they sat on the rock, coats pulled around them as the sun dipped towards the horizon, talking easily about nothing in particular, eating their sandwiches and drinking coffee. Josie had to admit, the view was spectacular, the sun's orange glow spreading across the wide expanse of Dartmoor as behind them the sky turned dark blue and then purple as the day slipped away.

'This was rated number three in best sunsets in the region by *Southwest Life and Times Magazine*,' Hilda said, 'behind Hope Cove in South Devon and Land's End. I've seen both of those, though.'

'Sounds like you're ticking off a bucket list,' Josie said.

'Something like that. Another one is seeing my best friend happy.'

'Well, you can tick that box. There were a few teething problems, but things are moving pretty smoothly now.'

'Lovely that Tiffany came down to stay,' Hilda said. 'She seems to have fitted right in. I sometimes wish I'd had children.' She sighed. 'I was always too busy. Never gave myself a minute's break from work.'

'If it makes you feel better, I sometimes think of you as a surrogate mother.'

'Oh, you're too kind.'

'You've done so much for me, though. If you hadn't forced the issue, I'd probably still be living in my cousin's flat.'

'No, you'd have done something. You've always had that kind of warrior spirit. I knew you'd be all right if I could just get you down here. And look at you now. The campsite is looking great. When is it you're planning to open?'

'Tiffany said we should aim for the first of June.'

'Do you think you'll be ready?'

'It's going to be tight. We still have a fair bit of maintenance work to do, and we haven't stocked the shop yet, but Tiffany said we've already got a few bookings.'

'That's great news.'

'I'm lucky to have a daughter capable of doing all the online stuff, while Lindsay, Geoffrey and Barney have been great around the camp. Then there's Robinson … he's done so much around the place when he's been available.'

'He's a lovely man.' Hilda grinned. 'You should flutter your eyelashes at him a little more.'

Josie felt herself blushing. 'Don't be ridiculous. Tiffany was saying the same thing. I'm just not … not ready. And anyway, I don't think … we're not really suited, are we? He's a … what, a handyman? He's so practical. I'm not. I mean, I'm—I was—a teacher. I've spent my whole life indoors. He looks like he spends half his life on the beach. I spent half of mine in a darkened room.'

Hilda patted her on the arm. 'Oh, Josie, you always assume so much. You know what he does for a living, don't you?'

'Fixes things?'

'I admit that he's got a knack for it. He installed the water lights in my pond and also repaired the frame around my mock Tudor entrance, but that's just for a bit of spare change when he's got nothing else on.'

'That's not his job?'

'Goodness, no. He's a geologist.'

'A … geologist? Like, a scientist?'

'He works for University College London, where he lectures. I think it's exam period at the moment, which is why he keeps going back upcountry.'

'Huh. And I was—'

'A geography teacher?'

Josie smiled. 'Yep.'

'I don't know what it is about the modern world, but people are always so afraid to ask questions that they prefer to just assume the answers. He's a geologist; you're a geography teacher. You're more or less the same age, and you're both single.' Hilda grinned. 'And you're both divorced.'

'Are we?'

'Nat was telling me. She was a lecturer too, got offered a position in Edinburgh. It turned out one of the other lecturers up there was more than just a colleague.'

'Oh my.'

'And he has a son, Steven. He's in the second year of a business degree at Reading University. Robinson often stops in to visit him on the way back down to Cornwall.'

'Do you make notes on people?'

'No, I'm just getting old. I'm not afraid to gossip because what does it matter to me anymore? I like to know about people, so I ask. Everything these days is filtered through a screen, people only giving up what they're willing to tell, and expecting that other people are exactly the same.' She clenched a fist and tapped it three times against the rock. 'Just … ask … questions.'

'All right. Why did you really need to walk all the way up here just to look at the sunset? And why did you want me to come?'

Hilda's smile dropped. 'I suppose I shouldn't push my views on people quite so hard, should I? Ask the dog enough times to bite and it will, and all that.'

'Come on. Share.'

'Isn't the sunset beautiful? I mean, it's everything I expected it to be and more. Wouldn't it be great if you could get those colours to streak in the petals of a rose?'

'Hilda…?'

The old woman wasn't listening, however. As the sun

started to dip below the distant horizon, colours fanning around it as though it were melting into the moor itself, Hilda climbed down from the rock, shouldered her bag, picked up her stick, and started off back down the hill.

'Come on,' she called over her shoulder. 'We really should be getting back to the bike. It'll be getting dark soon, and I'm not as mobile as I used to be.'

For a few seconds, Josie just watched her friend's back, before she gathered up her things and started down.

What was up with Hilda? For a woman so insistent that Josie be open and share her feelings, she had locked her own behind a closed door.

Something was wrong, Josie could feel it.

19

THE NEED TO BURY ONESELF

'You look hungover.'

Tiffany gave Josie a bleary-eyed smile and tucked a strand of loose hair up under a tall woollen hat that resembled a tea cosy. 'Don't you know, hangovers only affect people over the age of thirty. I prefer to call it "lack of the required amount of sleep". Had I not been so dedicated to my work, I would still be hiding under the covers.'

'Good night at the pub?'

Tiffany grinned. 'What happens in The Horse and Buoy, stays in The Horse and Buoy. You know that, Mum. But let's just say that when you add farmers to fishermen and sprinkle a little cider over the top, you get mayhem.' She gave an emphatic swipe of her brow. 'And I thought Fresher's Week was a wild party. Ain't no party like a Cornish fishing village party.'

'I'm glad you're enjoying yourself. Nice hat.'

'Cool, isn't it? I got it in a craft shop just up the road from the pub.'

'Don't you have enough hats by now?'

'There's no such thing as too many hats.'

'Are you sure it's actually a hat? It's got holes.'

'They're artistic.'

Josie smiled. 'If you say so. What's on the schedule for today?'

Tiffany's smile dropped. 'Oh, the drama. Someone from the council's coming in to check the septic tank and the sewage pipes from the shower and toilet block. Got to get that form stamped, Mum.'

'How are we paying for this?'

'I secured us a small loan.'

'Really?'

'Don't worry, I've used your half of the sale of our house for collateral. It's all good.'

'What? Aren't I supposed to sign for something like that?'

Tiffany pulled a sheet of paper out from under a pile of other sheets of paper, a seemingly jumbled mess. She poked a finger at a box at the bottom of the scrawl of legal jargon.

'Yep. Right here.'

'Tiffany—'

'It's all good. We just need the collateral. Nat said you're good to clear it out of the profits, Hilda's offered to cover it if necessary, and … drum roll?'

'Huh?'

'Wave your hands about a bit, please.'

Josie flapped her hands in the air and made a drum sound that made her feel like a performing turkey despite the chuckle it brought from Tiffany.

'And … from September I'll be making the big medical bucks. I've applied for a residency spot at a place in Plymouth. William—Rachel's fiancé—said he'd put in a good word.'

Josie let out a little squeal. 'Oh, that's lovely. So, you're going to go back?'

'I can't waste five years of studying, can I? Although I might be going pro rata. Not sure I can handle the full-time hours. Plus, I've also got an eye on one of those international positions, you know, helping out kids in Africa, something like that.'

Josie wiped away a tear. 'I couldn't be prouder of you, Tiffany.'

Tiffany's smile dropped again. 'Do you want the bad news? Or, well, I suppose good, depending on your perspective?'

'Slap me in the face with it.'

'Dad's song is at number one. Like, in the whole country.'

Josie couldn't help but smile as she gave a disbelieving shake of her head. 'Good for him.'

Tiffany lifted an eyebrow. 'Him and that aristocratic troll posted a celebratory dance on TikTok.' She pulled a phone out of her pocket. 'Do you want to see?'

Josie put up a hand. 'Absolutely not.'

'It's got two-million views already. Honestly, some people have no taste.'

'Each to their own. Anyway, I'd better get to work. Today's plan for little me is to make an inventory of the cabins and list of what needs to be replaced.'

'Oh, I had a chat with Cathy in the pub. She said if you want to get a laundering service going on for the cabin linen, she'll do you a deal, since you're "a babe."' Tiffany lifted an eyebrow. 'I assumed she meant you look good for your age, rather than that you're an actual child.'

'Um, that's good I suppose.'

'And she said she had some cousins looking for a place to camp for the summer holidays.'

Josie spread her hands. 'The more the merrier.'

'Did you know that Rachel delivered one of her children? Right there on the launderette floor.'

'The things that happen in small towns, eh?' Josie clapped her hands together. 'Right, I'd better get back to it.'

'Oh, and Robinson called. He asked if you needed any more wiring done.'

'Ah, I think we're good for now.'

'Mum?'

'What?'

'He's totally looking for excuses to come down here.'

Josie shook her head, turning away so as not to meet her daughter's eyes. 'He doesn't need an excuse. His dad owns it.'

'Come on, Mum. Just make it easy for him.'

'I don't know what you're talking about.'

'Oh, you do. You're just being difficult. Come on, it's the summer! It's the time for romance!'

'It's still May. That's technically spring.'

'Oh, Mum….'

Josie left the reception cabin before Tiffany had a chance to corner her. The air was fresh, warm even, the ground a little damp after some overnight rain.

She found Geoffrey and Lindsay together, painting the outside of the play barn, laughing gently at some in-joke to which Josie wasn't privy. Barney was down by the treehouses, hanging a rope swing between two of the platforms of the treehouse village. For several days last week, all five of them had got together to repaint the outsides of the treehouses, the sides blue and green, the roofs in polka-dot red and orange, like a series of mushroom houses clinging to the trees. Robinson had come down to help Barney build a couple of stairways leading up, and the walkways and barriers had all been repaired.

Josie carried on down to the clearing, where she stood for a moment, looking out over the cove and the cliffs below. Tiffany, working her magic, had got the council to commit to repairing the section of the coast path below the campsite, and even to cut a series of steps leading down to the secretive cove. While it was never going to be a top swimming beach or ideal for making sandcastles, it would make a good setting for a few beach barbeques and maybe a little fishing.

She was just thinking of going down for a wander on the beach when she heard Tiffany shouting her name. She walked back up through the campsite, unable not to feel a sense of amazement at how much it had changed from an overgrown wilderness into something that actually looked habitable.

Hilda was waiting outside the reception shed. She had driven her open-backed van down and still wore wellies and a pair of gardening gloves. In the back of the van were several lines of planter boxes filled with an assortment of flowers.

'Ah, Josie, there you are. I was clearing out one of my greenhouses and thought of you.'

'What's all this?'

'These are a few of my own varieties, some that are public, others that are still in culture. I thought you could use them to border the access road. I have a friend who rents out those miniature diggers you can get for landscape gardening. We can put them right up to the main entrance. Of course, it's your project, but I have some ideas for the colour schemes.'

Josie wiped away a tear. 'That would be lovely.'

Hilda grinned. 'Since some of these varieties are unique, I could get you a bit of press in the gardening magazines. Believe it or not, there are people who'd visit just to see these flowers. And of course, I can provide you with seeds to sell in the shop.'

'That would be great. Thank you so much.'

As Josie stared at Hilda, a sudden wave of emotion flooded over her. Her vision blurred, and she found herself sobbing.

Through the strength of friends and family, new and old, things were coming together. It was really working.

Hilda was hugging her. 'It's just a few flowers,' she said, almost admonishing Josie. 'It'll look a bit better than brambles and nettles, that's all.'

'Why are you being so kind to me?'

'I'm just helping out a friend, and to be honest, I've got no room for all of these. I need to start clearing things out.'

Josie pulled back. 'What do you mean? Are you planning to move or something?'

Hilda looked down, not meeting Josie's eyes. 'I'm getting old,' she said. 'It's time to downsize, that's all. I can't manage it at my age.'

'Are you sure?'

'Yes. Stop worrying about me. I'm an old workhorse.'

Josie was about to say something else, when a familiar voice hailed them. Robinson came walking down the lane, grinning as he lifted a hand to wave.

'Not too late, am I?'

'For what?' Josie said, a little more sternly than she had anticipated, getting her a sharp look from Hilda for her troubles.

'Hilda called me and said you had some stuff to unload,' he said.

Josie looked around and saw Tiffany standing by the door to the reception cabin. When she saw Josie looking, she just shrugged.

Was this some kind of conspiracy to push them together? Suddenly she felt a little queasy.

'I'll be back in a minute,' she said, turning and fleeing back through the campsite to the shower block. She went into a toilet cubicle and sat down, holding her face in her hands. She couldn't do it; she just couldn't. Even if by some miracle Robinson did like her, the thought of getting burnt again … she just couldn't go there. The whole country was currently dancing to a song about what a terrible wife she had been. Wouldn't it be better to just put her head into the ground and forget about everything? Perhaps dig a hole big enough that she could fall inside, be covered over, and never be seen again? Maybe Reid would come up with a sequel to his hit song, detailing her death. At next year's Glastonbury Festival, maybe a hundred thousand people would sing along.

She was just wondering whether she could flush herself down the toilet when she heard Barney shout her name. Josie went back outside, looking around. She caught a glimpse of movement in the trees nearby, Barney waving her over.

'Josie, quick, come over here. I've found some kind of hole.'

20

PLOT HOLES

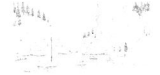

BARNEY WAS STANDING among the trees a little off the main path down through the campsite, holding a tree branch which he had stripped of leaves. As Josie arrived, he held up a hand, waving her back.

'Don't come too close,' he said. 'I don't know how big it is. It's down there, in among the roots of that tree.'

The hole was a dark hollow in the shadow of a towering pine which had tilted slightly, perhaps damaged in a storm long-ago. A couple of feet wide, the hole sloped steeply into the earth. As Barney poked at the edges with a stick, a lump of sod broke away from one side, widening it by a few inches.

'I was just having a wander about and I spotted it,' Barney said. 'Don't remember seeing it before.'

'Could it be a badger set or a fox den? Maybe a rabbit warren?' Josie, wanting to be hopeful, knew she was wrong even as she offered the suggestions. The angle of the hole, plus the lack of any material removed nearby, made it clear that nothing had dug it out. Some subterranean space had been covered over, and the tree roots had gradually unearthed it.

'It goes right down,' Barney said, leaning forwards and poking the stick inside. It went in five or six feet, but Josie put up a hand to stop him as he inched closer, trying to find some kind of bottom.

'Careful,' she said. 'It could go right under our feet for all we know.'

The ground felt solid enough, but if the cave or whatever was this close to the surface, they could be standing on its roof. Any sudden movement and it might collapse.

'I'm sure it wasn't there before,' Barney said. 'I was clearing the brambles around here a couple of days ago and I don't remember seeing it.'

'We need to cordon it off,' Josie said.

'There's a bit of rope left over from the swing,' Barney said. 'I'll go and grab it.'

As he hurried off through the trees, Josie stared at the hole in the ground. Just the look of it, the way the ground had crumbled around the entrance, gave her a bad feeling. How big was it? How far back did it go under their feet?'

She had an instinctive sense that this was bad news. At the very least, they had to fill it in, make sure no kids playing hide and seek came across it and decided to climb inside. Who could tell how deep it was?

Barney came back with the rope. Together, they strung it around the trees nearby, giving the hole a wide berth.

'I think it's best if we keep this quiet for now,' Josie said. 'Don't tell anyone outside the park. I'll get Tiffany to have look online, see if we can find out what it might be.'

'I'm sure it's not very big,' he said, but from the way he gave an uncertain shrug followed by a sheepish grin and a shake of his head, Josie could tell he was just as worried.

She headed back up to the reception cabin, where

Tiffany was talking with Hilda. The flowers had been unloaded, the planter boxes set out in neat rows along the front of the cabin. Josie looked around, feeling a pang of disappointment when she didn't spot Robinson anywhere nearby.

'He's already gone,' Hilda said, giving her a sympathetic smile.

'Who?'

'You know who,' Hilda said, as Tiffany rolled her eyes and scoffed. 'Robinson. He had to go. He said he's got some event up in London this evening, so he had to go over to Plymouth to catch the train.'

'I had to … go too,' Josie muttered.

'Don't worry, he'll be back in a few days,' Tiffany said with a chirpy grin. 'Don't look so glum.'

'It's not that,' Josie said. 'We … Barney … found something in the woods.'

'If it's a corpse, we can just roll it into the sea,' Hilda said with a chuckle. 'Same with an abandoned car. Or we could just make it into a horticultural feature.'

'It's not a corpse, or an abandoned car,' Josie said. 'In fact, I'm not sure what it is. Come on, I'll show you.'

She led Tiffany and Hilda into the woods. At the sight of the rope, Hilda let out a gasp. 'Not a hornet's nest, is it?'

'I don't think so, but you never know what might be inside.'

'Inside what?'

'There.' Josie pointed over the rope at the hole in the earth.

'It's probably just an animal burrow,' Tiffany said.

'That's what I thought, but what animal round here burrows something two-feet wide?'

'Could be a Sasquatch,' Tiffany said. 'Or a giant land sloth.'

'Don't joke.'

'It's probably just a depression caused by the tilt of that tree, or water run-off, something like that.'

Josie looked at Hilda. The older woman was staring at the hole, face grave, seemingly unconvinced by her own words.

'What if it's a cave that connects to the sea?' Tiffany said.

'Unless you're talking about some ancient prehistoric sea a hundred yards closer, then we're much too far off for that.'

'So, what do you think?'

Hilda rubbed her chin. 'I think we need to go and have a word with Nat, see if he has any of the land deeds or surveyor's maps. It could be some old excavation, perhaps an old construction project that was never finished.'

'Do you really think so?'

Hilda forced a smile. 'I'm sure it's nothing to worry about. You're not planning to open for a few weeks, anyway, are you? Plenty of time to sort it out.'

Josie glanced at Tiffany, who gave a dramatic shrug.

'Perhaps when we dig out the verge for those flowers, we should save some of the soil, in case we need to fill it in?'

Hilda patted Tiffany on the shoulder. 'There's a good, practical idea. I'm sure it's nothing to worry about. Shall we go and have a cup of tea? Or better still, an ice cream down in the village?'

'This could be serious,' Tiffany said with a smile. 'I don't think anything less than fudge cake topped with ice cream will be sufficient to get us through this. We'll need a full team briefing, too. We can take Lindsay, Geoffrey and Barney.'

'Somehow I get the impression you aren't taking this seriously,' Josie said.

'It's probably the site of ancient pirate treasure,' Tiffany said.

Hilda forced a smile, but when Josie looked at her, her friend quickly looked away, as though she didn't quite share Tiffany's flippancy after all.

'So, I suppose this is as good a time as ever,' Lindsay said, patting Geoffrey's hand as they sat facing the others across the little table in the Sunset Harbour Coffee and Fudge Company. Several large slices of fudge cake loaded with ice cream sat between them, like concrete tank barricades on a beachhead topped with foam. 'We've decided that we're going to get married.'

Tiffany let out a squeal of delight, so sudden that one of the old ladies behind the counter jumped, hitting her head on a hanging saucepan.

'How lovely,' Hilda said. 'Congratulations to you both.'

'That's wonderful,' Josie added.

'We'd like to have the ceremony at the campsite, in the clearing where we first met,' Geoffrey said. 'On Midsummer's night.'

'Is that safe?' Tiffany asked. 'Isn't that when ghosts and stuff come out?'

'Only in fairy tales,' Geoffrey said.

'Well, if there really is a St. Michael out there in the cove, perhaps he'll give us his blessing.'

'I'm sure it'll be lovely.'

Lindsay smiled, then suddenly burst into tears. As Geoffrey consoled her, Josie snatched a serviette out of a holder on the adjacent table, while Tiffany jumped up to grab a box of tissues off the countertop. Hilda, meanwhile, took advantage of the distraction to scoop a lump of Lindsay's ice cream onto her own plate.

'What?' she said, shrugging at Josie. 'They gave her loads more than me.'

Josie just rolled her eyes and turned back to Lindsay as Tiffany thrust the box of tissues into her hands.

'My family are going to come,' Lindsay said. 'My two daughters, my mother and father, and my brother. We're working through what happened, and they've decided to forgive me. They're all going to stay at the campsite for the week. I've told them all about the trees, the beach, the views … they're so excited.'

'We'd better get a move on and get it ready then,' Tiffany said, lifting her coffee. 'The clock's ticking, so bottoms up.'

It seemed like something of a paradox that what was technically nothing would play so much on her mind, but Josie couldn't keep the hole out of her head. She wanted to believe Hilda, that it was just a run-off channel or the remains of an old excavation project that had never come to anything, but from the way her friend had looked, she knew Hilda wasn't convinced either.

Wanting to take her mind off things, she let them all have the afternoon off, and they decamped to the pub for a couple of drinks. The sky was clear, the air warm, so they took a table out in the beer garden. Josie offered to go and get the drinks, while Hilda agreed to accompany her.

Inside, The Horse and Buoy was more of a museum than a pub, historical artefacts displayed on shelves alongside dusty black-and-white photographs of the parish in times gone by. Fishing images and relics dominated, but there was also place for several old farming photographs of horse-drawn ploughs, ancient threshing machines. Josie found herself staring at a picture of a stone tower on a clifftop, set dramatically against a backdrop of the English Channel. When she turned to Hilda, her friend was staring at her.

'You know what that is, don't you?'

Josie turned back to look at the picture. Had it been a little shorter, it could have been a church, but it was a simple stone design, too tall to be practical as somewhere to live or worship, a functional building perhaps, no windows, no obvious features other than its narrow shape.

'It's a pumping tower,' Hilda said. 'They used to be everywhere around here, but the few that are left are derelict now.'

'Pumping tower. You mean for a—' Josie's breath caught. 'That isn't what I think it is, is it?'

Hilda grimaced. 'I'm afraid so. I really didn't want to say anything because … well, I have my reasons. But that hole … the problem we have could be bigger—much bigger than you think. Around here … this is mining country.'

21

POSSIBLE SOLUTIONS

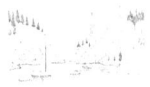

'Over there, someplace,' Nat said, gesturing vaguely in the direction of the gravel pile in the corner of his driveway. 'Didn't need it all, did they? Feel free to scoop up a few buckets. Just heave 'em in. Nothing a bit of gravel won't fix. Shove a bit of soil over top and you're back in business.'

'It could be more serious than that,' Hilda said. 'If it really is part of a mine shaft, it'll need a bit more than a few buckets of gravel.'

Nat just grinned. 'Take the whole pile if you's need.'

Hilda looked at Josie and sighed, then looked back at Nat. 'Are you messing with me, Nathaniel?' she said in a stern, schoolteacher's voice which made Josie a little envious. 'You know this is serious, don't you?'

Nat grinned. 'Do I look like I'm joshing with you's, maid?'

'Yes.'

'Nat planted one hand on his scrawny hip and lifted the other like he might ask for a drink. 'Hil, you know I'd never mess with you's. Look, if it does fall through—I mean, the site, not you's, maid—' Nat broke into a few seconds of spontaneous laughter so infectious that even Josie cracked a smile. '—then it's no great loss, is it? Just cut the grass back a bit. Had a crack, didn't work out. All good.'

Josie had a sudden outburst of anger. 'We've put weeks of work into that campsite,' she said.

'Maid, sometimes you's have to walk away. I remember exactly when I knew me days as a cult leader was up. Just woke up one morning, and things felt a bit iffy. Had to go for a walk, and never went back.'

Before Josie could answer, Hilda said, 'Not everyone feels as "free" as you, Nat.'

'Ah, more's the pity,' Nat said. 'Be way less bees getting in bonnets if 'twas true. Look, just have a go with the gravel. If you don't have enough, or he keeps pouring down, have another think.'

Nat returned to the sculpture he was halfway through carving, a quite exquisite waterboard of mermaids rising out of a stormy sea. Humming to himself, he began to chip away at the driftwood with a chisel as though they had already gone.

Josie and Hilda looked at the pile of gravel, then dismissed it with a wordless shrug. They climbed into the truck and headed back to the campsite, neither with much to say.

AFTER HILDA DROPPED her off at the campsite entrance, Josie walked down the lane, finding Lindsay, Geoffrey and Barney hard at work planting Hilda's flowers, following colour layouts they had all got together to plan a couple of days ago. The radio Nat had given to Josie sat on the grass between them, playing a summery tune. As Josie reached them, the three together lifted their heads and bellowed out the chorus:

'With you, my dear, hand in hand, walking together 'cross the summery sand—'

'That's nice,' Josie said. 'I don't know that song.'

'It's a local station,' Barney said. 'Tiffany told us not to play the main ones. Something about a licencing thing on commercial properties.'

'Is that so?' Josie said.

'Do you think Lindsay should go with a traditional white or a spring pale pink?' Geoffrey said, looking up, his hands and knees covered in sodden mud. 'We can't decide.'

'Um, I don't … whatever you think will look best,' Josie said.

'I don't think it matters,' Lindsay said. 'We have the perfect place, the perfect date. Jeans and a t-shirt would do.'

'You've got to wear a dress,' Geoffrey said. 'What about bright red? Something that'll crash the ships out in the Channel.'

'Don't be silly.'

Geoffrey grinned. 'What about we celebrate how we met and you wear a grass skirt?'

'We were only dressing like that because we were off the grid,' Lindsay said.

'What about something cotton? That's a plant? Call it a compromise.'

'Gets my vote,' Barney said. 'You know, as best man and everything.'

'You're the best man?' Josie asked.

Lindsay smiled. Josie stared at her a moment, still unable to come to terms with the change. Lindsay was shedding years on a daily basis. She was talking regularly to her family via video call and had introduced them to Geoffrey and Barney. Even Josie and Tiffany had said a quick hello.

'We'd like you to be a bridesmaid,' Lindsay said.

Josie nearly choked. 'What?'

'At our wedding. We'd like you, Tiffany and Hilda to all be bridesmaids.'

Josie lifted an eyebrow. 'Is that an acceptable average age for bridesmaids?'

'It's is now. Tiffany said she can't wait to start shopping for matching dresses, although she was a little disappointed when I said she couldn't wear a hat. Maybe a tiara or something. I think you'd all look lovely with them.'

Josie grimaced. 'Right. Well, I need to go and have a word with her. Thanks for doing the flowers.'

She found Tiffany in the reception cabin, hunched over the computer.

'What's this about commercial radio use?' Josie said.

Tiffany looked up and grinned. 'Oh, that. I had a look online, and picked the only station that doesn't have Dad's song on its A-playlist. I thought you'd appreciate it.'

'Ha, thanks. You shouldn't lie to the staff, though.'

'Radio South Coast Cornwall has the best music anyway. A mixture of dodgy eighties hits and sea shanties.'

'Sounds wonderful. And what about going dress shopping?'

'Lindsay's going a little crazy over this wedding thing. I thought it would be great if we had matching dresses. Perhaps we can even make them ourselves?'

'We have less than a month.'

'Yeah, not so likely.' Tiffany's smile dropped. 'So … do you want the bad news?'

'It's about the hole, isn't it?'

'Uh huh.' Tiffany sighed. 'I've gone through the historical records, and can't find anything about a mine on this site, but that just means an actual working mine. There were speculatory shafts and tunnels dug all over the place, looking for ore seams, many of which aren't registered anywhere. What it does mean is that we'll need a land survey done, to make sure. Otherwise, if we open the campsite and there's an accident, we'll be in big trouble. At the very least we'll get shut down.'

'And let me guess … it's expensive?'

Tiffany whistled through her teeth and rubbed her fingers together. 'Did you know, Dad's song is now number one in France. Perhaps we could ask him for a loan?'

'I'd rather sell my underwear.'

Tiffany gave her a sour look. 'I doubt that'll pay for a survey, Mum.'

'So, what do we do?'

'Why don't we ask Robinson? Isn't he a geologist? He might be able to help.'

Josie grimaced. 'I'd rather not involve him. Anyway, he's up in London.'

'But he comes down every few days to check on Nat.' She picked up a newly installed dial phone. 'I can call Nat now, find out when he's back—'

'No!'

'Mum?'

Josie lowered the hands she had lifted as though vainly trying to ward off an approaching lorry. 'Look … I'll talk to Hilda about it. She'll know what to do.'

'She'll probably tell you to ask Robinson.'

Josie scowled. 'Haven't you got some web-designing to do?'

Feeling restless and unable to concentrate on any tasks needing to be done, Josie walked up to the main road, then back towards Porth Melynos, planning to drop in on Hilda.

Her friend's large house, sitting right at the top of the hill, had a spectacular view over the village and the harbour. Josie hadn't called ahead, thinking she would surprise Hilda, and picked up a couple of scones in a little bakery along the way, just to ease the shock. Hilda would likely be out in her greenhouses, tending to her multitude of plants, some of which existed nowhere else in the world.

Hilda always had time for her, and even though Josie didn't like to admit it, she always treasured Hilda's advice. She had so much more world experience. She would know what to do, about the campsite, about the hole, even about Robinson.

Just act like a river and go with the flow, my wonder. Don't fret it all so much.

Like a calming summer breeze, Hilda's voice was already playing in Josie's mind as she came around the last corner. It was what Josie needed; it would make everything better—

She dropped the bag of scones and let out a horrified shriek.

Outside Hilda's front door, where her gardening van and her motorbike were usually parked, stood a waiting ambulance.

22

HILDA'S SECRET

'Excuse me, what's going on?' Josie said, leaning through the ambulance's open rear doors. It was empty, but just as she was wondering whether to go into the house, voices came from the garden. Two paramedics appeared, carrying a stretcher, another jogging alongside. Josie let out another gasp at the sight of Hilda lying on the stretcher.

'What happened?' she gasped.

'Madam, please stand back,' said one paramedic, waving her aside as they made for the ambulance's rear doors.

'It's nothing,' Hilda said, turning her head and trying to sit up as the two carrying the stretcher lifted her into the back of the ambulance. 'Just a turn, that's all.'

'Can I come with you?'

'I'm sorry, madam,' said the first paramedic. 'Are you a next of kin?'

'I'm her best friend.'

The paramedics looked at each other. 'We're taking Ms. Lewisham to Derriford in Plymouth,' one said, as another shut the rear doors.

'Thank you.'

'Perhaps you could bring an overnight bag?'

Josie just nodded, face roaring with heat, as they climbed into the ambulance. Then, lights blaring and siren wailing, it sped away up the road.

Josie, hands shaking, pulled her phone out of her pocket. She tried Tiffany, but it directed immediately to voicemail. Starting to panic, she nearly dropped the phone, before remembering the landline Tiffany had installed in the reception. Her daughter had called Josie's phone to test whether it worked.

She searched her received calls list. There it was: an unfamiliar number. She quickly dialled it back.

'Good morning, Porth Melynos Caravan and Camping Park,' came a spritely voice. 'This is Tiffany speaking. How may I help you on this wonderful sunny day?'

It was just starting to rain. Josie gulped, her mouth dry. 'Tiff, it's me,' she rasped. 'I need a vehicle right away.'

'Mum, you sound terrible. Did you just rob a bank?'

Josie swallowed again. 'It's Hilda,' she said. 'She's gone into hospital.'

Tiffany let out a little scream. 'Where are you now?'

'Up on the main road. Do you think it would be okay to steal Hilda's van?'

'You're not insured, so give me five minutes to sort something out. Stay right there.'

'Don't worry,' Cathy Ubbers said, hammering the launderette van into another blind corner. 'I know these roads like the back of me hand.'

Josie grabbed Tiffany's knees in horror as Cathy suddenly let go of the wheel completely. The van swerved across the road with a squeal of the tires. The baseball cap Tiffany had been wearing bounced down into the footwell, Tiffany just managing to swipe it before it got in the way of the brake pedal.

'What's these? Oh, the backs of me hands!'

With a wild chortle, Cathy grabbed the wheel again and swung them sharply back into the hedgerow, narrowly missing an oncoming minibus. Josie caught a glimpse of the words Saltash Canoeing Club on the side and a half dozen or so terrified teenage faces pressed against the windows, then they were dipping down a meandering lane beneath overhanging trees.

'Are you sure this is the way?' Josie gasped.

'Shortcut, innit?' Cathy said. 'Don't worry, we'll be there, soon as.' She slapped Tiffany, sitting between them, on the thigh. 'So glad you called me, love. Always like to make meself useful. Hil, she's such an old dear.'

'Is it much further?'

Cathy grinned. 'Not if you know all the shortcuts.'

'I'm guessing you do?'

'Made half of them up myself, didn't I? Last time me and Gav were timing, we'd shaved six minutes off the usual route. You know what that means, don't you? Extra twelve minutes in Primark per shopping trip.' She rolled her eyes. 'Well, Gav wanted to go up Virgin Megastores, but I said, who buys CDs these days?'

'It's a good point,' Tiffany muttered.

'A good point,' Josie echoed.

'I mean, it's all streaming, innit? Like that song at number one. It's all just playlists and stuff, no one's actually buying it, are they? I mean, a song like that, some guy moaning about his wife, who'd pay money for that? What a plonker—woah, almost missed that tractor, didn't I?'

Josie found herself pressed against the window, Tiffany

leaning against her shoulder. The tractor passed, a blur of green and red, so close that clods of mud sprayed in through Cathy's open driver's side window.

'Watch where you're going!' Cathy shouted, picking a sod of muddy grass off the dashboard and tossing it onto the road. 'Can't you see we're ladies?'

Much to Josie's pleasant surprise, they reached Derriford Hospital some twenty-minutes later without any of them being sick or the car being involved in a head-on collision. Josie told them she wanted to see Hilda alone, so Cathy offered to take Tiffany on a Starbucks run.

'We'll get you a Frappuccino,' she called out of the window as the van pulled away, taking a wide-eyed Tiffany with it. 'Extra cream. You'll need it for the shock.'

Josie went into the reception and told the staff Hilda's name.

'I'm her best friend,' she said. 'I had just arrived at her house when I saw the ambulance. I don't know what happened.'

The receptionist asked her to wait while she made a phone call. A minute later she put down the phone and looked up at Josie.

'She's just having some tests done, but she'll be in the ward soon so if you want to, you can go over to the department and wait.'

'Yes, please.'

'Okay. The receptionist set a hospital map down on the counter and indicated the route Josie needed to take.

'Here, on the second floor.'

Josie looked up. 'Cancer … what do you mean? Why's she on the cancer ward?'

'I think you and your friend will need to talk about that.'

Josie hurried through the hospital to the cancer treatment department. Asking at a departmental reception desk, she was shown to a seat and told to wait. An hour and three cups of overly sweet machine coffee ticked by. She messaged Tiffany to say she'd be a while, and a reply came to say Cathy had taken her to Primark. Finally, a nurse came over and tapped her on the shoulder.

'Ms. Roberts? Ms. Lewisham is on the ward now if you would like to see her.'

Hilda, wearing hospital pyjamas, was sitting up in bed with a gardening magazine open on her lap. She looked less than happy, but smiled when she noticed Josie standing at the foot of her bed.

'I've already read this one cover to cover,' she said, giving the magazine a dismissive tap. 'Can you believe it's the most recent issue they have?'

Josie came over to the bed and put a hand over Hilda's, noticing to her shock the tube coming out of her friend's forearm.

'Oh, don't worry about that,' Hilda said. 'It's just a few vitamins and things. The same stuff I give to plants.'

'Why didn't you tell me?'

Hilda visibly sagged. 'Not the best conversation opener, is it? I meant to, I just … couldn't. I can't even admit it to myself. I've been a warrior my whole life. I've rarely even had a cold. And now … this.'

'How bad is it?'

Hilda sighed. 'Stage two lung cancer.'

'Stage … what does that mean?'

'It could get worse; it could get better. I might live; I might die. That's about what it means.'

'Lung cancer? How? You don't smoke; you spent most of your life around plants … it doesn't make sense.'

'There's one battle none of us can win,' Hilda said.

'The battle against time. I'm an old woman; that's about the be all and end all.'

'An old woman who rides a motorbike, climbs hills to look at sunsets—'

'Goes parachuting, don't forget that. Incredible experience.'

'It just doesn't seem possible.'

'I'm bucket-listing, aren't I? Just in case I'm no longer here this time next year.'

'Don't say that.'

Hilda sighed again. 'I was perfectly happy with my old Ford Mondeo. The motorbike was an impulse buy.'

'You should have told me.'

'I tried to, but you were going through your divorce and I didn't want you worrying about me on top of everything else. Then when you told me how you'd ended up, about selling the house and everything, I saw a chance to spend a bit of time with you. I knew your pride would stop you taking an extended holiday, but I remembered Nat's family's campsite and thought it would give you a project to keep you nearby for a while if I could talk him into letting you have a go.'

'Oh, Hilda. You should have just told me.'

'I know, I know, but I didn't want you fussing around me and worrying all the time. I'm perfectly all right. Well, apart from the Big C, but otherwise. I just had a turn, that's all. It was too hot in the greenhouse. Nothing to do with the cancer.'

'I don't believe you. Have you started treatment yet?'

'They said they have some more tests to do, but it probably won't be long.' She sighed. 'Can you have a word with Tiffany? I might need to borrow a couple of hats.'

23
LOOKING FOR HELP

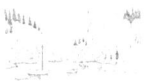

HILDA WANTED to keep her diagnosis a secret from the whole population of Porth Melynos, so Josie told Tiffany and Cathy that Hilda's diagnosis was inconclusive. While Tiffany gave her a sly look to suggest she knew a lie when she heard one, Cathy was thankfully more interested in the bargains she had found during their shopping trip. As she dropped them off, a little queasy but with stomach contents intact, at the top of the campsite road, Josie promised to fill her in on any updates. As soon as Cathy sped off, Tiffany turned to her.

'Cancer, isn't it?'

'Um, what?'

'Mum, I've just completed five years of medical school. Don't try to lie to me.'

Josie broke down all over again. Tiffany took her back to her cabin and made a cup of tea.

'She's my best friend,' she sobbed. 'I had no idea.'

'She said it's stage two, right?' Tiffany said. 'That means they've caught it in time. She might be fine. There's a good chance.'

'What if she's not?'

'Mum, we could both get hit by a bus—or a speeding launderette van, more likely—tomorrow. Even with cancer, she could yet outlive both of us. You have to be strong for her.'

Josie reached out and touched Tiffany's cheek. 'I'm so proud of you.'

'You keep saying that.'

'I know, but I am. Look at me, I'm barely keeping myself together. It should be the other way around.'

'Just think of Hilda. You need to be strong for her.'

'I'm doing my best. It seems like everyone around me is managing to cope with what life throws at them except for me. Why is that, Tiff?'

'I think you're doing okay. Just take a deep breath.'

Josie puffed out her cheeks. 'Right. So, one thing at a time, right? We have a campsite to open, but before we can do that, we have a hole in the ground to deal with. We can't afford a survey, can we?'

'Not without calling in a favour, getting another loan, or selling your underwear. None of which are great options, are they? Obviously the first one is the best, but we're not talking a tenner for fish 'n' chips. A survey on a plot this size could cost a hundred grand. Nat doesn't have it, neither of us have it, and the only person who might is Hilda, but do you really want to ask her?'

'I would rather sell my underwear.'

Tiffany rolled her eyes. 'Well, that's the first fiver sorted. What about the rest?'

Josie couldn't help but smile. 'We're screwed, aren't we? We're going to have to close down before we've even opened.'

'Not necessarily. Thanks to a bit of genius—if I do say so myself—with SEO and online advertising, bookings are going great. We're full a couple of weeks in August already, and I've applied for an on-site catering licence so we can flog some ice creams. You know that the profit margin is about sixty percent? Forget alcohol. Ice creams, cakes and scones are where the real money is. Then there's the tour excursions. I've got moorland trekking, sea-fishing, foraging, and even farming experiences pencilled in. Not to mention trips to local landmarks.'

'How on earth can you arrange all that?'

Tiffany tipped the pink baseball cap she wore, emblazoned with the slogan, *Cathy's Cleaning: You'll scrub up nice* across the front. 'I know a woman who knows a dog, and that dog knows everyone,' she said.

'You never cease to amaze me.'

'Well, to say thank you, I want you to do something for me. I heard from Lindsay and Geoffrey that Robinson's coming back down tomorrow morning. I want you to go over there and ask if there's anything he can tell us about that hole. He's a geologist after all.'

'Robinson … do I really have to involve him?'

Tiffany let out a frustrated groan. 'Mum, this is business. You don't need to go over there and flutter your eyelashes at him. Although it might help avoid a consultation fee. Take a clipboard or something and wear a t-shirt with paint on it or whatever. At least if he can give us an idea of what's down there, we'll be in a better position to succeed.'

'What do you mean?'

'We're only screwed if it's a mine. If it's a natural cave caused by the rock strata, we're in the clear. We'd only need to fence it off.'

'And if it's the entrance to a mine tunnel?'

'Then it's better that we find out now, so we cancel everything before financial penalties kick in.'

'Are you serious?'

'Don't be fooled by the hat.'

Josie finished her tea. It had gone cold, and left a sour taste on her tongue. With another sigh, she stood up.

'All right,' she said.

IT WAS hard to keep herself busy when the world was threatening to crash down around her, but she found that cutting the ivy away from the back of the play barn was suitably mind-numbing to fill the void of her life for a few hours. The next morning, with shoulders that felt like they'd been pulling trees out by the roots, she put off what she had to do until late-afternoon, then walked up to Nathaniel's house by the road route. There were still plenty of hours left in the day, but the sun already hung low over the hills to the west, casting its glow over the English Channel. The sky was clear, the air warm enough that she had to remove her jumper. The road rose to a viewing spot before dipping down again into the clifftop farmland where Nathaniel lived, and Josie paused for a moment to look out over the sea.

Staring at the wide blue expanse of the English Channel, she suddenly felt tiny, little more than a speck of dust, clinging to the side of a massive, spinning ball. The sea, the cliffs, the hills and the valleys, even the trees, would still be here long after she had become but a memory.

Why do we try so hard? Everything comes from nothing, returns to nothing. The foreground flashes in and out of focus, but the background barely changes. The players on the stage come and go, but the stage stays the same.

And then she thought of Hilda, lying in a hospital bed, still defiant. Nat, mole-blind, chipping away at his driftwood sculptures. Lindsay and Geoffrey, trying to repair years of personal failings. Even Tiffany, fresh out of medical school, initially jaded, but now rediscovering a bright-eyed sense of wonder.

Why not enjoy what we have? Live every moment for everything we are worth, and worry about what happens afterwards, after.

She lifted her hands and gave a sudden whoop, then cupped her hands around her mouth and let out a long, screeching howl.

It felt good. Like she was reaching inside herself, pulling something out. She cupped her hands to do it again—

'Are you all right?'

Her heart leapt as she spun around. She hadn't heard or seen anyone, but a man on a bicycle had pulled into the verge behind her and was watching her with an expression of both surprise and amusement. At first the floppy beach hat left his eyes shadowed, the afternoon sun on his face filling in the lines of his cheeks and jaw with colour, so it wasn't until he smiled and lifted the hat that she recognised him.

'Robinson? What are you doing here?'

He nudged the bag on his shoulder. 'Dad wanted fish 'n' chips,' he said. 'I'm just riding down to get him some.'

'Are you serious?'

'Ah, yes.'

'You're riding down that hill?'

He nodded. 'Then riding a little slower back up. You should try it. Gets the blood flowing. Actually, if you like I can give you a backie.'

'Excuse me, a what?'

'A backie. You sit on the seat with your legs out. I'll stand up and pedal. Didn't you ever do it at school?'

'I caught a school bus.'

'Ah, never mind. Come on. I can give up a lift down, but you'll have to walk back up. And that's no diss on your weight. Parts of that hill are one in six. I have to push the bike back up as it is. Twenty years ago, no problem, but I'm getting lazy in my old age.'

'You're not old.'

'I suppose it depends on the outside conditions. Compared to Dad, no. Compared to young Barney or your Tiffany, I'm ancient. Compared to you, perhaps—' He smiled, then quickly looked away. 'I'm maybe just right.'

Josie's cheeks burnt. *Live life*. 'A backie?' She took a deep breath. 'Okay, come on then.'

He helped her climb on to the bike. 'You'll have to hold on to me,' he said. 'Hold my waist, but don't squeeze too tight and try not to lean when we go round corners or we'll both come off. I'll try not to go too fast.'

Josie's cheeks burnt with heat, but at least he was facing ahead and couldn't see her. 'All right.'

Robinson, standing in front, took the handlebars and put his feet on the pedals. The bike, a solid-framed mountain bike with deep-treaded off-road tyres, wobbled under their collective weight as they started to move.

'Oh, god,' Josie muttered, grabbing hold of the hips of Robinson's jeans.

'Are you all right?'

'I'm terrified.'

'Just hold on. Put your hands around my waist and lean into my back if you get scared. Don't worry, you'll be fine.'

The road naturally sloped down into the village, so Robinson barely had to pedal at all. Holding on to the brakes, he took them gently down the coast road until they reached the outskirts of the village, houses on either side. The road widened and they passed a couple of cars coming the other way. Josie, hanging on for dear life, tried to enjoy the thrill of the wind in her hair as they freewheeled past expensive clifftop houses.

'Right, are you ready? Here's the fun bit,' Robinson said, as they came around a corner and found themselves at the top of the steep hill dropping diagonally down the hillside to the harbour below. A sheer stonewalled hedgerow overhung by trees made up one side. On the other was a line of cottages built into the hillside.

'Let's go,' Josie said, voice trembling.

'Are you sure?'

'Y … yes.'

'All right.'

Robinson pushed off again. For a few seconds they moved gently, like a rollercoaster reaching the top of its incline, then quickly accelerated, the noise of the wind filling Josie's ears. As their speed increased, she clung on tighter, the hill so steep she could barely muster the nerve to breathe. Robinson had one hand on the brake, but Josie nudged his arm.

'Faster!' she screamed.

Laughing, Robinson let go of the brake and they plunged into an apparent freefall, the houses flashing past them in a blur. Josie clung to Robinson, no longer pedalling at all but leaning forward over the handlebars as though to streamline them, send them rocketing even faster.

'*Faster!*'

Up ahead was a tight, switchback corner, beyond it seemingly only the sea. Josie let out a gasp in terror, certain now that Robinson meant to dissect a gap in the crash barriers, send them flying over the edge into oblivion. A call for him to stop bounced on her tongue, but none would come. She wanted to shut her eyes, but found them opening wider as she peered out from behind his shoulder, the wind billowing into them drying them open, freezing her vision on the potential disaster.

And then, with an expert twist, Robinson both braked and turned at the same time, hacking them around the corner. The world swung, Josie's stomach lurching, and she found herself facing the pretty village set into the valley as they dropped down the last section of the hill, gradually flattening out as it came to another corner and a hump-backed bridge over the river.

There was one last thrill as they bumped over the bridge, then they were coming to a stop outside a fish 'n' chip shop not far from the harbour.

Josie could barely move. Robinson stepped off the bike and turned to face her, his face ghost-white.

'I never went that fast even as a kid,' he gasped, running a hand through hair that was now hatless. 'Are you out of your mind?'

Josie grinned. 'I am now,' she said.

They ordered fish 'n' chips, then proceeded with a more sedate walk back up the hill, Robinson pushing the bike, collecting his hat from the branch of a low-hanging tree halfway up, while Josie walked alongside.

Exhausted by the time they got back to the viewing spot, Robinson suggested they sit down on a bench overlooking the sea to eat.

'What about your dad?' Josie asked.

Robinson grinned. 'We have a microwave. He was in the middle of a sculpture anyway. He won't mind. I'll just tell him there was a queue.'

As they sat side by side, their food on their laps, Josie

had a sudden moment of clarity that to all intents and purposes they were on a date. The freedom with which she had talked about nothing important on the walk up the hill deserted her, her tongue appearing to tie itself into an abrupt knot.

'It's … um … pretty.'

'The sea?'

'Yes.'

'What in particular about it?'

'Huh?'

'What do you particularly like about the sea to consider it pretty?'

'I—'

Robinson grinned. 'Don't worry. I'm just playing around. Relax.'

'I am relaxed.' *No, I'm not.*

Robinson just grinned as he detached a chip from the rest of the soggy clump and tossed it into his mouth.

'What's your favourite sea animal?' he asked.

'Favourite … I … never really thought about it. Ah … sharks?'

'Why?'

'I suppose because they're kind of like the boss of the sea. Nothing eats them.'

'Except us, and sometimes killer whales.'

Josie chuckled. 'I suppose that's true. So, you don't like sharks?'

'Oh, no, I think sharks are great. I just wondered what you thought.'

'Why? Is this some kind of personality test?'

Robinson popped another chip into his mouth. 'Nope.'

'So why ask?'

'Why not? All right. If you could do anything right now that involves water, what would you do?'

'Wash?'

Robinson laughed. 'I was thinking more like water sports. Surfing?'

'I've never tried it.'

'I could teach you. Although Dad was the master, back in the day.' He grinned. 'I am but an apprentice.'

'Isn't it scary getting smashed by big waves?'

'Yeah, but it's kind of exhilarating. You know, not dying. I kind of like it.'

'Isn't that what we're all doing, day after day? Not dying?'

'Of course, but we're not aware of it. Only when you stand a little closer to the edge do you realise how much you appreciate where you are.'

'And because we're not really aware of it, we drift and we drift, and suddenly, it's too late.' She couldn't get the image of Hilda, lying in the hospital bed, with a tube in her arm, out of her head. 'Sometimes … we have to say what we really feel, when we feel it.'

Robinson just gazed out at the sea, popping another chip into his mouth. 'You're relaxed now, aren't you?'

'Huh?' Josie laughed. 'I guess I am.'

'So, what is it you want to say? Don't be afraid. Just say it.'

Josie closed her eyes and opened her mouth, trying not to think about what she was going to say, but to let her tongue take on a life of its own. She remembered how it had been so easy in her late teens and early twenties, helped by a glass of wine or two. Now, at forty-five, with a lifetime of playing by the rules behind her, it was infinitely harder.

'My … I … I think … well … my daughter, and um, my best friend, have been trying to look out for me after what my ex-husband did.'

'The musician guy?'

'Yeah.'

Robinson nodded. 'I've heard about him. Tiffany was telling me. He's at number one, right? God, that song is terrible.'

Josie couldn't help but laugh. 'Yeah, him. Anyway, yeah, he was a scumbag, treated me like a doormat and basically used me for our entire marriage to push his career while burying mine, I was still for some strange reason in love with him.'

'Women love a bad guy. It's evolution, as natural as a rock formation.'

'That's … one way to look at it.'

Robinson just shrugged, ate another chip.

'Well, because of that, because he basically broke my heart, my soul, my resolve, and my emotional ability to deal with relationships—not to mention decimating my bank account—I just can't even think about another relationship right now, even if my daughter and my best friend think it would fix me.'

'That's completely reasonable.'

She turned to look at him. 'It is?'

'Yeah. Of course it is.'

'Really?' Part of her couldn't help but feel a little disappointed at his own seeming lack of disappointment. It was as though he had no feelings for her at all.

Why would he? I've basically run away from him at every opportunity.

'I'm a geologist,' he said. 'I study timeframes that are almost too incomprehensible for people to understand. 'Waiting isn't something that bothers me.'

'Waiting?'

'Yeah.'

She felt all prickly hot again. Did he mean waiting for her?

'What are you …waiting for?'

Robinson grinned. 'I'm waiting to see what happens. I don't believe in forcing any situation any more than necessary.'

'Right.'

They sat in silence for a couple of minutes. Josie stared out at the sea, analysing his words for hidden meaning. Robinson, however, just stared at the sea, without a care in the world.

Eventually, he said, 'So, what was it you were coming to see me about?'

'What? I—how did you know?'

'Tiffany called me to say you were heading up to Dad's place. I thought I'd come and meet you, save you the walk.'

'You were coming to meet me?'

'Yeah. And get Dad's fish 'n' chips, of course. Two birds, one stone, and all that.'

'But you didn't say.'

'No, because I thought you would. Eventually. See what I mean about waiting? I think we've reached that point where you're about to tell me, though.'

'It's about the campsite,' she sighed, shoulders slumping, all her whimsical wonderings crashing to earth. 'We might have a bit of a problem.'

24

EXPLORATION PARTY

Josie, Tiffany, Lindsay, Geoffrey and Barney stood nearby as Robinson secured the climbing rope around the tree trunk and fastened it with a carabiner before fitting it to his belt.

'Be careful,' Josie said, getting a nudge in her ribs from Tiffany, who wore a wide grin. 'What?'

'A pound says it's just an animal burrow,' Tiffany said.

'I'm going with the entrance to a secret government bunker,' Geoffrey said.

'A diamond mine,' Barney said.

Lindsay just gave Josie a sympathetic smile. 'I'm sure it's nothing.'

Robinson fed the rope out as he walked backwards to the hole. He wore a hard hat fitted with a light, while he had changed out of his casual clothes into climbing boots and overalls.

'Are you going to be all right?' Josie asked, unable to help herself, despite a snigger from Tiffany.

'No problem,' Robinson said, then began to feed the rope out as he lowered himself into the hole.

'You knew, didn't you?' Josie whispered, leaning close to her daughter.

Tiffany grinned. 'Of course. He's a certified caving instructor. It only took a minute or two of research to find out. Honestly, Mum, the internet would save you a lot of trouble if you figured out how to use it.'

Josie shrugged. 'Maybe next week.'

They watched as Robinson, pausing briefly to give them a wide grin and a thumbs up, slowly abseiled down into the hole. As soon as he disappeared from view, they all craned forwards, trying to see how far he had gone down, but in truth, all they could see was the rope jerking back and forth for a few seconds before suddenly going slack.

'Oh, God, what's happened?' Lindsay said.

'Robinson!' Josie shouted. 'Are you all right down there?'

'Mum, stop being so … *keen*.'

'All good,' came a faint cry. 'Just give me a minute.'

They waited, glancing nervously at each other. The rope hung slackly into the hole, and no further sound came from inside. Josie glanced down at her feet, wondering if he was right below her, or whether he'd stepped over some hidden precipice and been lost forever.

'Should we go and give the rope a tug?' she suggested, after a five-minute wait that felt like three hours. 'Perhaps he's hurt himself.'

'Just be patient, Mum. He's a professional.'

'I know, but what if he's—'

The rope went suddenly taut, and a moment later Robinson appeared, climbing up out of the hole. Halfway out, he unclipped the rope and turned to face them.

'Is that safe?' Geoffrey asked.

Robinson grinned. 'There are steps,' he said. 'I'm standing on them. It's perfectly safe.'

'Is it a mineshaft?' offered Lindsay.

'A sink hole?' Tiffany said.

'The entrance to hell?' Barney suggested.

'Treasure?' Geoffrey said, although he sounded more optimistic than the others.

'Are we going to have to close the campsite?'

Robinson lifted a hand, pointing at them one at a time. 'No, no, I don't think so, kind of, maybe temporarily. Josie, you're in charge of this place. Would you like to come down and have a look? I just need to get some more gear out of the van. We're going to need some bigger lights, plus a decent camera.' Then, while they all stared at him, he gave them a wide grin. 'Oh, boy. Just what have we found here? I'd brush your hair and perhaps change your clothes ready for *National Geographic*.'

'What is it?' Josie asked, as she trailed Robinson back up to the van with the others following behind, ready to help carry any equipment they needed.

'I'm not exactly sure,' he said. 'I'll need to do a little research.' He turned to look at her. The boyish grin on his face was intoxicating. He looked like a kid who had just discovered treasure buried in his back garden. 'Oh, what a great day it is.'

With Robinson literally humming to himself, he handed out items to each of them, then led them back to the hole.

'We need to be very careful,' he said, stepping over the rope and walking to the dark space below the slanting tree trunk. 'I'll take you all down one by one to have a look, but under no circumstances should you touch anything. Nothing at all. What we have here is … significant.'

He took Josie first. Wearing a hard hat with a light, she waited by the edge of the hole while Robinson went down to set up his lights. Then, when he re-emerged below her, he reached out a hand.

'Careful now. It's a little … ancient.'

His hand, even through the gloves they both wore, felt warm and strong. Josie gripped it hard as she descended into the darkness.

Robinson was right; there were steps. Just out of sight below the surface they began, lines of packed slate which over time had been covered over with earth. Narrow, barely wide enough for her to move without turning side-on, a few steps further down her headlight illuminated walls also made of stone. In places tree roots had bound or misplaced them, but as they descended deeper and deeper the invasion of vegetation became less and less. The stone walls, ancient beyond what she could perceive, looked as good as they might have done when they were built, however many years ago.

'How far down are we?' she asked Robinson as she came up behind him where he had paused at the bottom of the steps, stone flags underfoot.

'Twenty feet or so,' he said. 'Deep enough that there's no fear of the ground collapsing short of construction work.' He turned to look at her. In the glow of her headlight, he looked triumphant. 'Are you ready for this?' he asked. 'You get to see something like this for the first time perhaps once in your life. Are you ready?'

She nodded.

'All right. I've set up a couple of lights. Remember, don't touch anything at all. Not a thing. This place has to stay exactly as it is.'

'Okay.'

He reached out and took her hand, leading her forwards. They followed a short earthen-floored passageway lined by stone walls that rose just enough for her to walk without stooping. Overhead, stone beams were interspersed with the flaky remains of what might once have been logs.

'It's a little tumbledown up ahead,' Robinson said. 'Part of the ceiling has collapsed. Just step over the stones.'

They moved forwards again, even slower, and Josie saw he was right: part of the ceiling had fallen in, but there was still plenty of space to pass and even though she knew they were deep underground, with Robinson to guide her, she felt no fear, only a growing sense of excitement.

Finally, he paused at an opening. Behind it was some kind of chamber. Inside, he had set up a couple of floor lights to illuminate it with a dim, orange glow.

'Close your eyes,' he said, taking her hand again. 'I'll lead you.'

She did as she was told, shuffling forwards until Robinson squeezed her hand.

'Okay,' he said.

She opened her eyes. She stood in a chamber that was perhaps no bigger than the small living room at her old house, but here, in this ancient place, it felt vast. The ceiling was domed, roughly hewn stones and ancient, petrified wood all woven together. The walls were stone, and the floor was bare earth, dry and dusty, covered with an inch of dust and powdery dirt.

Lining the chamber were raised stone shelves, topped by all manner of ancient artefacts, cups and bowls and utensils, weapons, other items she couldn't even guess at. All were crude, clay or bronze, roughly made, showing signs of a long, slow decay.

A treasure trove of stunning proportions, the artefacts alone might have been enough to build a new museum, but the stone dais in the centre felt like a generational discovery. Waist-high and built of stone, atop it lay a skeleton, perhaps once dressed in ancient ceremonial clothing. Weapons by the person's sides identified him or her as someone of great significance, a king or warrior perhaps. However, even the skeleton was nothing compared to the two skeletons that lay on lower dais to either side.

'Is that … is that a lion?' Josie whispered, pointing at a skull that stood beside the feet of the human skeleton, as though some ancient prehistoric beast had lain down to die at its master's side. 'Isn't it a bit big?'

Robinson was nodding frantically. 'Yes, but no,' he said. 'We need to make a few phone calls, but as a basic guess, it looks like we have two complete skeletons of *Panthera spelaea*, more commonly known as the cave or steppe lion. They were significantly bigger than the lions we know today, but lacked manes.'

'It looks a bit … fossilised.'

Robinson was still nodding. He turned to Josie and took her hands in his, almost without realising it.

'We've just stumbled upon the archaeological find of the century. These animals went extinct around thirteen-thousand years ago. And while there have been occasional bones found this far south, the presence of two perfect specimens, suggests something altogether different.'

His excitement was infectious. Josie couldn't help but smile. 'Humour me.'

'They were … pets. Pets or guards, maybe, but almost certainly domesticated. Pets to a … king. A real live lion king.'

25

INVASION OF THE BOFFINS

The car park was full of lorries. As another came rumbling down the lane, Tiffany stepped out into its way and put up a hand. Josie, standing by the reception cabin, watched as her daughter opened her palm to the driver and said, 'Parking is a fiver per day.'

'Oh, right,' came a man's voice, and a hand stuck out, passing something to Tiffany. As the van rumbled on, Tiffany wandered over to Josie.

'Here's another,' she said, handing over a crumpled five-pound note. 'Add it to tonight's drinking fund.'

'How many is that?' Josie asked.

'Nine,' Tiffany said. 'Including the BBC journalists that showed up. Oh, and that guy from *National Geographic* wants an interview.'

'With me? Why?'

'He wants your first impressions of the cave,' Tiffany said.

'All right, well, I suppose we can schedule him in later. I have to go and see Hilda this morning.'

'Oh, and Robinson called.' Tiffany grinned. 'I think he wants to ask you out on a date.'

'I'm too old for that.'

'Mum, you know that middle age officially starts from fifty these days? That means that you're still young. Go on, do something crazy.'

'I'll think about it.'

Tiffany had some work to do on the computer, so Josie headed down into the campsite to see how the archaeological teams were getting on. The story hadn't broken yet, but Robinson had notified several of his scientist friends, and teams had come down from the British Museum and Oxford University, as well as the British Archaeological Society. Apparently the Cornish Archaeological Society were also on their way, but had stopped for pasties and a cream tea down in the village.

Everyone on site had been asked to keep the discovery quiet until the full extent of what they had found was known, but Lindsay and Geoffrey had already told her family, while Nathaniel was now frantically carving a life-sized sculpture of a cave lion out of a piece of driftwood for it to be placed at the campsite entrance.

Groups of boffins holding clipboards stood near to the cave entrance, while another group descended into the depths to video and photograph everything. So far, according to Robinson, nothing had been touched or moved, but eventually most of it would be taken away for study and testing. However, it was quite likely that a perfect replica would be installed in its place and the area turned into an open-air museum. Nathaniel had apparently already applied for planning permission to extend the access lane down into the forest.

'Hey.'

Josie looked up. Robinson stood nearby, looking dishevelled but excited. Since the discovery yesterday afternoon, it didn't look like he had either washed or slept.

'You look a mess.'

'I've been subsisting on ice cream for the last day or so. Sugar is the only thing keeping me awake.'

'Would a coffee help?' *What did I just say?*

Robinson grinned. 'I think it might.'

'Uh … I've got some at my cabin.'

'Sure.'

Josie found herself heading for her cabin with Robinson walking alongside. Her heart was thundering, trying to process what she had just said. The words had just slipped out, the connotations following after like a petulant child. As they reached her cabin, however, Robinson sat down at a picnic bench she had put outside.

'I'm not in the best of conditions right now,' he said with a grin. 'I don't want to get dirt on your carpet.'

'It's all right.'

Part of her felt relieved, part disappointed. She went inside and made some coffee, running over in her mind what she would say when she came back out. Tiffany said he had called for her. He seemed like a nice man, but was she really ready for any kind of involvement so soon after her divorce? Granted, she and Reid had been separated for years, but dredging it all up again for the benefit of the courts had left a sour—but expensive—taste in her mouth.

Even so, perhaps a few casual dates wouldn't hurt, if Robinson were really interested. She felt a whimsical thrill at the thought of walking hand in hand on the beach, sitting in cafés eating ice creams and drinking coffee together, and Robinson was certainly more interesting than most men she had ever met, including her ex-husband.

Perhaps she could give it a go. Maybe things would work out.

She had gained a little spring in her step as she came out of the cabin, carrying two steaming cups of coffee on a tray. *Just go with the flow, Josie,* she told herself. *Don't put any pressure on yourself.*

As she came down the steps from the cabin, however, she looked up and nearly dropped the tray in surprise.

Robinson was leaning over the table, head on his forearms, snoring soundly.

'So DO they think it's all real?' Hilda asked, sitting up in the hospital bed, popping grapes into her mouth one by one.

'According to Robinson, they've carbon-dated some of the bones back to around eleven thousand B.C.,' Josie said. 'It was previously thought that the cave lions died out near the end of the last ice age when their main food sources became scarcer. However, this discovery completely flips that, proving that at least some of them survived. Also, the bone structure of the two in the chamber is slightly different to those of any existing skeletons.'

'Meaning they were bred?'

'It looks like it. It could be one of the earliest known examples of animal husbandry.'

'Wow, that's amazing. What about the guy?'

'They think he was a tribal king of some kind. Some of the pottery has traces of rock only found much further north, suggesting the tribe might have been involved in some kind of invasion, or even trade.' She smiled. 'Robinson said—'

'It sounds like you've been spending a lot of time with Robinson of late.'

Josie felt herself blushing. 'We went for dinner last

night, in the pub. Just for him to give me a few updates on what's going on.'

'Updates,' Hilda huffed. 'Is that what you call it now?'

'Yes, just updates.' Even as she said it, Josie found herself smiling. 'Although … we shared a couple of glasses of wine too.'

'Just admit it. You like him.'

Josie shrugged. 'It's difficult not to like him. I mean, he's handsome, and he's so interesting. I'm just not sure … I'm not sure that I'm ready.'

'You deserve a bit of good luck after all you've been through.' Hilda put a hand over Josie's. 'I want to know that you're happy, before … before I die.'

'You're not going to die!'

'Well, not yet. But maybe it's not far off.'

'Don't say that. Have you got your results yet?'

'They're still running tests, but the doctor said I'll have to start treatment in the next couple of weeks. I'm afraid we won't be playing any games of table tennis for a while.'

Josie squeezed her eyes shut, not wanting to cry in front of Hilda, but a rogue tear slipped out anyway, fleeing down her cheek.

'Got something in your eye?' Hilda asked.

'Yeah,' Josie said, sniffing.

'Don't worry about me. I've done my time. If the clock is about to run out, that's fine. I've done everything I could have wanted with my life. I have no regrets. Except … well, I wanted to do the Eden Project zipline. Together.'

'You really must be out of your mind. I'd have a heart attack halfway across. Probably not even that far.'

'But what a way to go out.' Hilda sighed. 'It's got to be better than this.'

It was Josie's turn to pat Hilda's hand. 'Just stay strong,' she said.

26
SELF-EXCAVATION

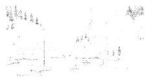

WHEN SHE GOT BACK to the campsite, she found a television crew from the BBC milling around in the car park outside the reception cabin. Tiffany was standing with Lindsay and Barney, shaking her head as Nat, still wearing sunglasses, grinned as he talked into the camera, a microphone making an indentation in his beard.

'It's like a surprise sandwich, isn't it?' he was saying to a mystified interviewer. 'You've got your historical bread on one side—that's the lad in the chamber over there—and you've got your modern bread on the other—me, of course. What's gonna be in the filling, well, that's just pot luck, isn't it?'

'What's happened?' Josie asked.

Tiffany grinned. 'They took a DNA sample from the ancient king, and compared it to Nat's. It turns out there's an eighty-percent match, meaning Nat could be a direct descendent.'

'Don't we share more DNA than that with gorillas?' Josie said.

'Don't tell them that,' Tiffany said with a grin. 'He just

spent half an hour telling them his family history, and how his cult days in the eighties must have been a subconscious attempt to restart his ancient tribe. At this rate we're looking at a two-hour documentary at least.'

'Well, I suppose I'd watch it if it came on.'

'By the way, what do you think of this?'

Tiffany reached into a plastic bag she was carrying and pulled out a pair of soft toys that looked like stocky, maneless lions. One was a dark, Halloween orange, the other slightly lighter. They both had spongy sabre-teeth and angry slanted eyebrows.

'Mr. and Mrs. Cavey,' Tiffany said. 'The park's—and quite possibly the village's—mascots.'

'Mr. and Mrs. … Cavey?'

Tiffany shrugged. 'It's a work in progress. It's pretty hard to find an original name using the word "lion". They've all been copyrighted.'

'What about the king?'

Tiffany reached into a bag and pulled out a stuffed doll with a bald head, a big beard, and clothes that reminded Josie of a Roman legionary, with the exception of the incongruous felt sunglasses covering its eyes.

'It … ah … looks like Nathaniel.'

Tiffany grimaced. 'It's still very much a work in progress. He insisted on the sunglasses and the loincloth. When I pointed out that the Ice Age was several thousand years before the Romans, his response was something along the lines of "emmets ain't gonna know".'

'That was a pretty good impression.'

Tiffany's eyes widened and she swung her head from side to side. 'Thanks. I'm working on it. Do you want the other good news?'

'Sure.'

'Due to the potential significance of what we've

found, a few of the big societies are going to group together to pay for a full land survey, so we're in the clear for that.'

'Great. Will we be able to open by mid-June, and more importantly, before Lindsay and Geoffrey's wedding?'

'Looks like it. Although we're going to have to do a bit of jostling for position. The southwestern corner of the park where the chamber was found will be cordoned off while excavations take place. There's also talk of a visitor centre and a small museum, although that might be somewhere in the village due to planning restrictions.'

'How exciting.'

'Isn't it great?'

'It really is.' Josie gave Tiffany a hug, but as she pulled away, she noticed a frown on her daughter's face.

'Mum, are you all right?'

Josie nodded. 'I'm fine. Really.'

'Are you sure?'

She gave Tiffany a smile, but it felt forced. 'Yes, really.'

'Mum?'

'Don't worry about me. I'm just worried about Hilda, that's all. Everything else is fine.'

She knew it wasn't, but she couldn't quite define what it was. She walked down through the campsite, smiling politely for each group of people that she passed, pausing to answer a few questions about her own limited involvement, playing the good host where she could, but she couldn't shake a nagging feeling that something was wrong.

She went back to her cabin, made a cup of tea, then sat for a while at the little bench, trying to work out just what it was that was troubling her.

I'm here, I'm surviving, and everything is going well. The campsite is on track, my daughter is nearby, my best friend is getting the treatment she needs, and I even have a man who seems to like me. So, what is it?

Something was there, niggling her, sitting right at the edge of her peripheral vision, like a little goblin, refusing to be banished into the dark. Josie sat for a while, drinking her tea, staring out of the cabin's little window at the forest beyond, letting her mind wander, her thoughts drift, trying to identify just what it was that she couldn't shake off in order to move on with her life.

Then, suddenly, it came into view.

And she knew what she needed to do.

SHE MADE an excuse to Tiffany that she had to go back up to Bristol to deal with some business for a couple of days. It wasn't true, and the look in Tiffany's eyes suggested she knew, but her daughter knew her well enough by now to just accept her mother's decision.

Wanting to do everything by herself—not just to prove that she could, but because she wanted to avoid being talked out of anything—she caught a bus from Porth Melynos's single bus stop up to the local railway station, and caught a train back to Exeter, and from there on to Bristol. Back in the city, she took another bus up to her old house, where the FOR SALE sign stood slanted in the overgrown square of front garden.

The house looked forlorn and unloved, devoid of the lustre it had once had, as though with no one living there anymore it had faded into sepia. Josie, feeling a little sense of disappointment, kicked away some brambles and gamely straightened the sign. Then, taking one last look at the house in which she had thought she had been happy, she turned and headed into town.

It didn't take long to find a record shop. It gave Josie a brief sense of satisfaction to see that in the new chart, Reid's single had dropped out of the Top Forty. She picked up a CD with a REDUCED sticker on the front and took it to the counter.

'A leaving present for my boss,' Josie muttered to the girl behind the counter, who gave her a knowing smile. 'I'm about to resign.'

She put her CD into her handbag and headed across Bristol to the smart part of town where Reid now lived with his new woman, Lady Evangeline. It had been remarkably easy to find her address online, and as Josie sat under a bus shelter a little way down the bright, leafy suburb road, she wondered how she might feel if and when she saw her ex-husband again.

It was a typical early summer's day in Bristol, a couple of degrees warmer than Cornwall, less wind, but still the constant overhead threat of rain. As she sat there, a fat dark cloud obscured the sun, and Josie waited for a cloudburst. It never came, however, the cloud passing on, the sun reappearing, the warmth to the air returning.

She took the CD out of her bag, turning it over in her hands. It still had the plastic wrapping on it, so she tore it off and opened the case. On one side of the cardboard slip case was a picture of her ex-husband standing with his acoustic guitar beside a stone humpbacked bridge out in the countryside. To her dismay Josie realised it was a picture she had taken herself some years before, back in their happier days, when their weekends had been taken up with trying to promote Reid and his music, booking shows, painstakingly making amateur promotion videos for his songs, taking mood photos anywhere and everywhere, trying to find a good look for someone not particularly photogenic.

She hadn't known about his music when they got married. It had been his 'secret thing', a little hobby he did from time to time. Only after their vows had been said did she discover just how big a part of his life it was, bigger, perhaps, than any other, and that she would never truly be a part of it, just something floating on the periphery, allowed to look in from time to time.

Tiffany's arrival had been a good excuse to keep her weekends for other things, but she had always sensed a resentment, that Tiffany should indeed also be placed second to Reid's career aspirations, and that Josie should perhaps carry the infant around while she held the camera or made phone calls to local bars and clubs. Her reluctance to put her daughter second to his dreams had marked the start of their marriage's slow decline, but it had taken years before the final death knell sounded. Now that it had, the only thing preventing Josie from moving forwards with her life was how she felt.

She stared at the picture. There had been good times, for sure. That had not been one of them; they had argued in the car about locations, and Josie had ended up missing a coffee date with a friend because Reid—determined to get a bridge photo—couldn't find one that suited him. It had been a long, boring day of bickering, all for one solitary photo.

Now, as she turned the CD case over in her hands, reading the lyrics printed on the inside flap, she realised that she no longer felt anything. She took a black marker pen out from her purse, pulled off the lid, and scrawled, *Goodbye, Reid, thanks for the memories,* on the side of the slip case. Then, standing up, she dropped it into a litter bin nearby.

The sun had come out, the late May air warm and

fresh. She hoped it boded well for the oncoming summer, but you never really could tell.

She decided to walk back into town. With a spring in her step, she shouldered her bag, gave a little smile, and set off.

Tiffany, Hilda and the campsite needed her.

27
HOMEWARD BOUND

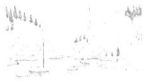

Hilda was sitting up in bed, a drip in her arm, a magazine open on her lap.

'You're looking a little better,' she said, as Josie pulled a chair close to the bedside.

'It's me that should be saying that to you,' Josie said. 'How is everything?'

Hilda shrugged. 'I start treatment tomorrow,' she said, reaching out to touch Josie's arm. 'I'm scared, Josie. I don't think I've ever really been scared before. Like, there was the time I was collecting samples in Africa and got chased down by a leopard, or the time in Antarctica when the sea started to freeze around the boat, but those were more exhilarating than genuine fear. I never thought I was going to die. I didn't realise how much I liked being alive until now.'

Josie held Hilda's hand. It lacked the strength it had once had, as though Hilda were slowly slipping away, and there was nothing either of them could do.

'We'll do that zipline,' she said. 'I promise.'

A tear ran down Hilda's cheek. 'Go and be happy,

Josie. Don't let the past define you. It's time to start building your future.'

Josie tried to reply, but all she could do was put her hand over her mouth in a pathetic attempt not to cry.

∽

'I WONDERED when you were coming back,' Tiffany said as Josie came through the door into the reception cabin. 'Look at all these.'

Lines of cards, soft toys, flowers and other random gifts filled every available space. 'Congratulations!' 'Good luck!' 'Happy Opening Day!' and more slogans shouted at Josie in gaudy, flamboyant lettering.

'Someone sent us a bread maker,' Tiffany said with a grin. 'I've always wanted one of those.'

'I didn't think people did things like this,' Josie said, shaking her head.

'Welcome to the modern age,' Tiffany said. 'You didn't forget that we open tomorrow, did you? Bookings have doubled since the excavation went public. Our first night, and we're already full. Biggest campsite in southern Cornwall.' She grinned. 'By the way, how does it feel to be immortalised?'

'Um, what?'

Tiffany's smile dropped. 'Didn't you hear?'

'Hear what?'

'Ah, that's right, you were off-site for a couple of days. There's been a pretty mental development.'

'What?'

Tiffany adjusted the straw hat she wore and made a drumming motion in the air. 'Drumroll, please—'

'Just tell me!'

Tiffany beamed. 'Ha, well, that guy in the tomb … it's not a guy.'

'Not a … what is it then?'

'It's a skeleton of a woman. The scientists think it could be the earliest known example of a warrior queen. And of course, for merchandising and general exploitation purposes, they needed a decent name.' She grinned. 'Nat and Robinson both agreed on it. Queen Josephine, Lady of the Cave Lions.'

Josie coughed. 'Are you having a laugh?'

'I think it has a lovely ring to it. Named after the first woman to set eyes on her.'

Josie shook her head. 'Oh my goodness. That's not something I expected. Is it too late to change it?'

'Yep. It's already being reported in the press. By the way, I put in an offer on a vacant commercial property down in the village, you know, getting in ahead of the expected price boom. It's right on the main street, and has a little flat upstairs, two bedrooms. I thought we—but mostly you, since I'll be doing my residency—would need something to do in the off-season. Plus, great job that you've done notwithstanding, this is still Nat's campsite.'

Josie smiled. 'My miracle daughter. How would I survive without you?'

'You'd manage. You did before. Coffee, trinkets, confectionary. What do you think?'

Josie took a deep breath. 'Queen Josephine's Café and Bookshop,' she said, trying the words out for size. 'How do you think that would sound?'

'I think it would sound perfect. Good choice, Mum.'

'I guess that puts paid to that Nathaniel lookalike doll,' Josie said.

'Nat's bought the entire stock already,' Josie said. 'He

said they're collectors' items. Do you want to see the prototype for Queen Josephine?'

'Do I want to see it?'

Tiffany smiled and pulled a soft toy doll out from under the counter. It looked vaguely Amazonian in a spongy, gaudy way, with one paw-like hand gripping a plastic spear.

'It's a work in progress,' Tiffany said. 'There's a bit of refining to do.'

Josie gave Tiffany a hug, then went down to the excavation site, wanting to see how things were going. It looked more like a construction site now, with plastic sheet fences erected around the site to keep the general public out. The scientists had created their own lane through the trees which emerged behind the reception cabin, but when she knocked on one of the plastic wall panels, someone appeared to let her inside.

There was a general buzz around the people milling about, an infectious excitement that made Josie smile. She watched for a few minutes, then took her leave, heading back up through the campsite to the main road, then along to Nathaniel's place.

Nat was outside, working on his life-sized carving of an ice-age cave lion. So far, he had only done the head—the body still a gnarled lump of driftwood—but his attention to detail and mastery of proportion were startling.

'Are you sure you're really blind?' she asked after greeting him, getting a chuckle from Nat in response.

'Just guiding the Lord's hand,' Nat said.

'Is Robinson around?'

'Inside, scribbling something down.'

She knocked on the shack's door, calling Robinson's name. He responded from somewhere inside, and she went in, stepping through the airy, cluttered interior until she saw him, emerging from a bedroom door, his hair neatly combed, a pair of spectacles perched on his head. For the first time that she had seen he wore clean, neat clothing, a pair of grey trousers and a pale blue shirt and tie. He reminded her a little of Harrison Ford in the few Indiana Jones university scenes, a rugged explorer come home to briefly roost.

'Josie.' He smiled, warm and welcoming. 'Sorry not to come to the door. I was just on a video call with Harvard University.'

She coughed. 'Really?'

'Yes, but I'm done now. Coffee?'

'Please.'

She followed him through into Nat's cluttered and cramped kitchen. In addition to the usual crockery and utensils, piles of pretty stones and shells covered the work surfaces, while bits of old fishing net hung from the walls. Some small fish and clumps of seaweed—which may have been decoration, may have been food—were hung up near a grimy, salt-clad window.

Robinson located the coffee and boiled the kettle. In the little cubicle space they were thrillingly close.

'I heard Cathy Ubbers is planning to change the launderette's name,' Robinson said.

'Really?'

'The Lion-drette,' he said.

'Are you serious?'

'She is,' he said. 'Queen Josephine is going to change the whole face of this village. You don't mind, do you? It was the first name that came into my mind when they asked. Dad agreed, and it stuck.'

'Do I mind you making me immortal? Not at all.'

'I'm glad.'

'You said it was … the first name that came into your mind?'

Robinson turned to face her. Behind him, the kettle started to bubble. A seagull squawked from the roof above them, its feet scraping on the corrugated iron roof.

'I've kind of had you on my mind a lot lately,' Robinson said.

'I've … been thinking about you, too.'

'Is that right?'

Josie nodded. 'I wondered if you wanted to … you know, get a drink?'

Robinson held up two mugs. 'I'm guessing you don't mean these?'

'That would do for a start.'

They were face to face. He was a little taller, three or four inches, but it was a good difference, just enough. Josie's heart was thundering, her stomach filled with butterflies. It felt good, a feeling she hadn't expected she would ever feel again.

He lifted a hand, but his fingers rested on her elbow. She watched him as he leant forwards, face serious, eyes flickering across her face as though studying her. Only inches separated them—

A crash came from the other room, and they both jerked away. Josie wiped her brow, and Robinson turned back to the boiling kettle.

'Lad? Lad, you in there?' came Nat's voice. 'Anyone seen me crayons?'

Robinson looked at Josie, then gave a wide smile. 'Can you make the coffee?' he asked. 'I'd better go and give him a hand.'

28
GRAND OPENING

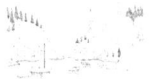

NATHANIEL HAD SUGGESTED FANCY DRESS, but Robinson had talked him down. Instead, as they stood together outside the reception cabin, they looked more set for a day on the beach. Nathaniel, Robinson, Geoffrey and Barney wore sandals, shorts and Hawaiian shirts, while Josie, Tiffany and Lindsay were light summer dresses with floral patterns and wide-brimmed straw hats.

A bright pink streamer hung across the entrance road, tied between two trees. On the other side stood a handful of locals, including Cathy Ubbers, Tiffany's friend Rachel, the landlord of the pub and the two old ladies who ran the fudge shop. Beside them were the scientists currently excavating the lion chamber, as it was now called, none of them looking particularly amused at being pulled away from their work. Beyond the group, backed up the road, were half a dozen cars and camper vans, the first customers, required to wait until this ceremony concluded. Several had got out of their vehicles and come down to join the small crowd.

'Right, let's get this over with,' Nat said, picking up a

pair of gardening shears—Josie's tearful representation of the absent Hilda—and stumbling over to the tape, Robinson close by, one hand on his elbow.

'Been a bit of a shambles, really,' Nat said, as the crowd hushed around him. 'Didn't think I'd ever see the day when my old man's pet project got back off the ground.' He paused for dramatic effect, then cackled with laughter. 'And I didn't, did I?'

A handful of people who got the joke laughed with him, but the rest had no idea he was blind. Nat raised the shears into the air.

'Big thanks to Hilda, who's not with us—ha, I'd have heard her nagging if she were—for convincing me to let her friend take a chainsaw to my patch of forest. And thanks to Josie—whom I believe is here somewhere—for doing such a good job.' He grinned. 'At least, so I'm told. Now, without any more fussing about, I declare the Porth Melynos Caravan and Camping Park open for business again.'

He swiped at the tape with the shears, missing it entirely. A second slash nearly took out Robinson's eye, but the third time he managed to get it. The tape split in two, the pieces fluttering away, and a cheer rose from the crowd. Robinson led Nat back to the verge outside the reception cabin, and the first vehicles rumbled onwards into the customer car park.

'And we're open,' Tiffany said, putting an arm around Josie's shoulders. 'Good work, Mum.'

'I couldn't have done it without you,' Josie said, looking at Tiffany. Then, glancing at Geoffrey, Lindsay and Barney, she added, 'I couldn't have done it without all of you. Thanks so much for all your work.'

Everyone was in a celebratory mood, but there was work to be done. The campers were coming thick and fast, and needed signing in, taking to their pitches, shown the facilities and local amenities. Realising they would quickly be overwhelmed, tomorrow was scheduled for interviewing for part-time workers. Running a campsite, Josie now realised, was no easy task. Still, with a welcome barbeque planned for tonight, and no chance of rain for at least the weekend, then Lindsay and Geoffrey's wedding planned for the following weekend, the party would continue for a while yet.

As everyone ran to their stations, Robinson came over to where Josie stood, watching the campervans and caravans come bumping into the car park.

'Great work,' he said. 'I had every faith in you.'

'Of course you did,' Josie said. 'I had every faith in myself.'

It was easy to lie about it now, but it felt far easier looking back on the bumps in the road that she had overcome, rather than the ones she was yet to face.

'I imagine from now on you're going to be pretty busy,' Robinson said.

'Flat out,' Josie replied.

'That's too bad.'

'But even so … I imagine even lion queens have to take a break sometime.'

'I'd think so,' Robinson said. He watched her, a smile on his face. 'You know, there's a nice little restaurant right by the harbour that does the best seafood on the English Channel,' Robinson said. 'If you did have time for a break, say, the day after tomorrow, perhaps you could find yourself there around about six o'clock? There's a little table by the window overlooking the harbour, which is the most popular, and really hard to reserve.'

Josie lifted an eyebrow. 'You seem to know it well.'

Robinson grinned. 'It's where I did work experience, all

those years ago. It's still there, though, and I managed to get a reservation, the only free spot until the end of August … next year. It would be so disappointing to eat there alone.'

Josie studied him. 'I'll see what I can do,' she said.

He held her gaze for a moment, the sun illuminating a warm smile on his face. 'I'll be waiting.'

THE CAMPERS CAME in a steady stream, and soon the park was full. It seemed as many had come for the archaeological discovery as for the beach, with half a dozen asking if they were doing guided tours within an hour of opening. With excavation work in progress, however, the best Josie and Tiffany could do was offer them a viewing of a video filmed inside the chamber with a voiceover by Robinson, followed by an ice cream with a flake shaped a little like a spear, and a photograph next to a life-sized carboard cutout of a cave lion, which Tiffany had ordered from the internet. And while Tiffany was keen to have Josie don fancy dress, so far she had resisted.

As another customer thanked them and head back to their tent, Tiffany put an arm around Josie's shoulders.

'You did it, Mum,' she said.

Josie shook her head. 'No,' she said. 'We did it. We all did it.'

Even as she said it, though, she couldn't help but think about what was missing, and a tear beaded in the corner of her eye.

29

LIKE A BIRD

I can't believe I'm doing this. As the instructor clipped the last carabiner to Josie's harness, she took a deep breath, trying to calm her thundering heart. From where she stood, the domes of the Eden Project looked so small, so far away, so far below her, while in front of her was only an arcing slope of wire that stretched out over the valley, so long that its distant end looked no thicker than a spider's web.

Josie gulped again. A warm August sun beat down on her, making her brow bead with sweat.

I can't believe I'm doing this.

She looked over her shoulder. Tiffany and Robinson stood there, watching her. Robinson had a wide grin on his face, while Tiffany looked distraught.

'Mum, you don't have to, you know.'

'I know,' Josie gasped, her throat dry. 'But I promised Hilda.'

'She really wouldn't mind if you pulled out,' Tiffany said.

Robinson chuckled. 'Oh, she would.'

'If this is goodbye, then you can have all my stuff,' Josie said to Tiffany. 'And Robinson … I'll miss you.'

He grinned. 'See you on the other side.'

'Ms. Roberts, are you ready?' asked the instructor with a grin. 'It's like flying. You'll feel like a bird.'

'I hate flying.' She took a deep breath. 'Let's go.'

'Go, Mum!' Tiffany shouted, while Robinson, due to go next, just laughed and clapped his hands.

The instructors pushed her off. The wooden platform dropped away beneath her feet, and suddenly Josie treasured the feel of something solid beneath her like nothing she ever had before. Then, she was flying, racing along the wire at a terrifying speed, the ground far below rushing by beneath her, the wind buffeting her hair, chilling her neck. Her legs and arms flailed and she let out a howl that was both terror and excitement. It really was like flying; she had become a soaring bird.

And then the end was approaching, and Josie realised she didn't want it to end, that she could indeed fly forever. As the wire dipped and the ground came up to meet her, she looked among the assembled people for the face she wished she would see more than any other, and she knew it was time for her flight to ground. As the instructors unclipped the harness and she stumbled jelly-legged away, people nearby clapped and cheered.

'Hilda,' she sobbed, the tears coming now, sobs shaking her chest. 'Hilda … where are you?'

A cackle of laughter came from behind her. 'Oh, Josie, my wonder, I'm right here.'

Josie spun around, nearly losing her balance as a wave of dizziness overcame her. She reached for a nearby fence post to steady herself, eyes scanning the faces nearby.

'Right here, dear.'

Josie turned. Hilda stood behind her, face pale as she

lifted her face to smile. Josie could never have said Hilda looked well, but since her positive result at the beginning of the month there had been a definite change. The hair might have gone, hidden beneath one of Tiffany's hats, but the smile had returned.

'How was it?' Hilda asked, as Josie pulled her into a hug.

'Absolutely terrifying, yet absolutely wonderful at the same time.'

'Next time I'll be coming with you,' Hilda said with a defiant smile. 'My treatment ends next month. It might have to be spring before I'm strong enough, but there's a marathon I've got my eye on next March. Are you going to join me?'

Josie laughed. 'I'll think about it.'

'Don't think, just do.'

'I'll think hard,' Josie said, laughing, still buzzing from the simple thrill of being alive. 'Right. It's lunch time soon. We'll just wait for Robinson and Tiffany, then we'll find somewhere to eat. What are you planning to have?'

Hilda grinned. 'Everything,' she said.

'Sounds good. I'll have one of those, too.'

END

THANK YOU FOR READING!

Summer in Sunset Harbour is the fourth book in the Glorious Summer series, and the eighteenth CP Ward romantic comedy overall. Have you read them all?

It has been my pleasure to bring these books to you. If you'd like to see more books from me and help them reach more people, please get in touch, tell your friends, neighbours, work colleagues. It all helps to spread the word! I dream of one day seeing Hollydell, Brentwell, Christmas Land, Sunset Harbour and others on the TV screen, so if you know someone in the business, give them a nudge! And in the meantime, share these books wherever you wish: online on your social media, at your book clubs, in the supermarket.

See you next time. CPW.

ABOUT THE AUTHOR

CP Ward is a pen name of Chris Ward, the author of the dystopian *Tube Riders* series, the horror/science fiction *Tales of Crow* series, and the *Endinfinium* YA fantasy series, as well as numerous other well-received stand alone novels. In addition, he writes the critically acclaimed *Slim Hardy Mysteries* under the name of Jack Benton, stories about cricket (the sport) as Michael White, and dinosaur apocalypse as Benton Ford.

A native of Cornwall, England, Chris has lived in Japan for the last twenty years, where by day he works in public elementary and middle schools.

He was once rejected for a Masters Degree in Creative Writing. He has since written more than sixty books and sold more than 200,000 copies. Never let anyone tell you that you're not good enough.

Summer in Sunset Harbour is the fourth book in the Glorious Summer series.

Expect more soon …

Chris would love to hear from you:
www.amillionmilesfromanywhere.com
chrisward@amillionmilesfromanywhere.net

Printed in Great Britain
by Amazon